Wild in Winter

The Wicked Winters Book Six

BY
SCARLETT SCOTT

Wild in Winter

The Wicked Winters Book Six

ISBN: 979-8-613882-62-5

Edited by Grace Bradley
Cover Design by Wicked Smart Designs

For more information, contact author Scarlett Scott.
www.scarlettscottauthor.com

Gill, the Duke of Coventry, has never been the sort of gentleman who woos ladies with effortless ease. In fact, he's never even kissed a woman, let alone courted one. But as the new duke, he's in need of a wealthy bride to replenish his dwindling familial coffers. Preferably a sweet, calm bride who is equally reserved. A bride who is nothing at all like Miss Christabella Winter.

Christabella is looking for passion. She longs for forbidden kisses in hidden alcoves, for a dashing rake to sweep her off her feet. Therefore, her dratted infatuation with the shy Duke of Coventry makes no sense. Particularly since he cannot be bothered to speak to her in complete sentences.

When she inadvertently learns the duke has never been kissed, however, Christabella forms the perfect plan. She can show him how to win a lady's heart and kiss him out of her system at the same time. But the problem with kisses is they often lead to something more, and soon, the only heart she wants him to win is hers.

Dedication

Dedicated to the Sassy Readers. You guys are the best!

Very special thanks to my sister and to author Caroline Lee for early reads of this manuscript and additional insight.

Chapter One

Oxfordshire, 1813

$\mathcal{M}$ISS CHRISTABELLA WINTER was in a terrible mood. A terrible, dreadful, horrid mood.

She cast a glance over her shoulder to make certain none of the guests at the country house party being hosted by her brother and sister-in-law wandered in the hall. Assured of her solitude, she crossed the threshold of the small, cozy salon where she had taken to hiding herself at Abingdon House. With its eastern-facing windows, generous hearth, and overstuffed chairs, it was the perfect place to indulge in an hour or two of uninterrupted reading.

She sighed as she closed the door at her back. Judging from the way her day had gone thus far, she may need a good three hours of pleasant diversion to distract herself from the grimness of her disposition. First, she deplored cold. Second, she did not like snow. Third, she was tired of playing charades, especially when none of the players could correctly guess what she was attempting to enact. Fourth, she had set her heart upon finding a wicked rake of her own at this cursed house party.

Instead, all the rakes had eyes for her sisters.

Which left Christabella with no one, the only hope of entertainment to be had in the small, leather-bound volume she had secreted in the hidden pocket she had sewn into her gown for just such a purpose. Because the book she was about to read was not just any book. No, indeed. It was a volume in the forbidden, wicked, utterly bawdy series of books known as *The Tale of Love*.

On another sigh, she threw herself into one of the chairs by the hearth, plucking the book from her pocket. At least she was assured of some rakish diversion within its pages, even if this house party had proven deadly boring thus far. She flipped to the page where she had last quit reading, toed off her shoes, tucked her feet underneath her bottom, and settled in.

That was when she heard it.

A noise.

The clearing of a masculine throat, to be precise.

She stilled, her eyes flying about the chamber.

And that was when she saw *him*.

The tall, golden-haired, infallibly handsome Duke of Coventry. The only man present at the house party who had yet to speak a word to her, not even during their introduction. He stood at the opposite end of the chamber, staring at her, his mien forbidding.

He looked, unless she was mistaken, as if he were vexed with her.

But how silly, for she was the one who ought to be nettled for the manner in which he was trespassing upon the salon she had claimed for herself. Why, it was all but her territory. He had no right to be here. None at all.

"Your Grace," she said, forgetting she ought to stand, slip her shoes back on, and curtsy. "What are you doing in my salon?"

His brows rose, as if he questioned her daring. But he said nothing.

What a queer man he was. Never mind that. He could

stand there all stoic and silent as he liked. She could talk enough for the both of them.

"Oh, of course," she said, frowning at him. "It is not *my* salon. But I have been reading here for the past few days, and I rather fancy it mine now. You will have to go somewhere else. Just look at how comfortable I have made myself in this chair. Do you dare disturb me?"

His nostrils flared. But still, he did not move. And still, he did not speak.

She wondered if it was because she had yet to observe formality.

"Must I curtsy?" she asked him. "It feels frightfully foolish to do so when we are the only two in the chamber. Just imagine us curtsying and bowing with no one to watch, when we are already committing an egregious faux pas by being here alone together."

His jaw seemed to harden, and the hands at his sides flexed. They were the only signs he was man and not a statue fashioned of coldest stone.

"Very well." On an irritated sigh, she flounced her gown and rose to her feet. "I shall curtsy. But do not expect me to put my slippers back on. They are too tight. I think they belong to my sister Grace. Her feet are a bit daintier than mine."

She dipped into a mocking curtsy, holding his gaze all the while. "There. Are you satisfied now, Your Grace?"

Finally, at long last, his lips moved.

He spoke.

One word, curt and definitive. "No."

She pursed her lips, studying the aggravating man. "That was a perfectly acceptable curtsy, I will have you know. One does not need to wear slippers in order to curtsy."

"Do you always talk this much?" he asked then, quite

rudely.

She blinked at him. "I think I liked you better when you were silent, Your Grace."

Then, the strangest thing happened, right there before her. The Duke of Coventry smiled. And her heart kicked into a gallop. *Good heavens*, he was the most handsome man she had ever beheld when he smiled that way.

Until he quite ruined the effect by speaking once more.

"The feeling is mutual, Miss Winter."

She could not contain her gasp of outrage. "That was impossibly boorish."

He stared at her some more. Was he ogling her stockinged toes? She wiggled them on the chance it would vex him. Once more, he said nothing.

She sighed then. "Are you not going to offer me an apology, Your Grace?"

"Why should I?" he asked. "You insulted me first."

Well, yes, she supposed she rather had.

At least he had deigned to speak again, so that had to count for something. A victory of sorts, however small. He was no longer smiling, but her body was still beset by the same irritating reaction to him. Her heart pounded. Her insides felt as if they were fashioned of warm honey. Worst of all, the wicked longing she felt in her core whenever she read *The Tale of Love* was throbbing to life.

She could not possibly be attracted to such a man. He was quiet and somber and socially inept. She adored rakes who were charming and knowing, with devilish grins and practiced kisses. Sinners and seducers.

The Duke of Coventry belonged to neither of those, she reminded herself firmly.

"The insult I paid you was a response to your ill-mannered question," Christabella pointed out. "It is not done to speak of a lady's discourse. You see? That is the way of a conversation."

His lips twitched. "Is it now?"

She had the strangest impression he was laughing at her. No one laughed at Christabella Winter.

She drew back her shoulders and pinned him with her most ferocious glare. "Yes. It is. Of course, I suppose one cannot expect a gentleman who shuns the society of others to know the proper rules of conducting a dialogue. Up until now, I confess, I wondered whether or not you were even in possession of a tongue."

He stiffened, and she regretted the harshness of her words.

But it was too late to call them back. They had been dropped between them, as sure as any gauntlet.

MISS CHRISTABELLA WINTER was dreadfully garrulous.

Horridly bold.

Insufferably rude.

She spoke to him as if she had not a care that he was a duke. And mayhap she did not.

Gill had come to the chamber to escape his hostess's idea of merriment. Charades made him want to retch into the nearest chamber pot. Mostly because the thought of all the eyes in the house party trained upon him simultaneously tangled his stomach in a vicious knot. Set his heart racing. Made his palms sweat and his chest hurt.

Also, because charades was a foolish game.

But he was a foolish man, because here he stood, engaging in a debate of sorts with a flame-haired hoyden who had insulted him. It was true that he needed the Winter family's coin to save his estates from certain ruin. A potential alliance with one of the Winter ladies had been his sole reason for attending this cursed country house party. But it was also true she was not the only unwed lady in England with a plump purse. He could easily find another. There was no need to waste his time by lingering here with her.

Except, the moment she had said the word *tongue*, he had been beset by the wildest surge of lust he had ever experienced. And as a man who had never even kissed a woman, he experienced more than his fair share of pent-up lust. This, however, trumped everything which had come before.

It was incapacitating.

More incapacitating, even, than his affliction.

For an indeterminate span of time, he could neither move, nor speak.

"Forgive me," she was saying, her voice bearing a tinge of contrition. "That was unpardonably rude of me to say. I cannot imagine what came over me, Your Grace."

She dropped the book she had been clutching to the cushion she had risen from. And then, she was moving, blast her. Coming nearer to him, her blue gown gliding softly about her. Bringing with her the scent of sweet summer blossoms and soft, delicious, tempting woman. Still, he could not move.

Or speak. He was beset by a strange combination of his affliction and raging desire. Why for this particular, vexing creature, he could not say.

"Oh, dear," Miss Winter said, stopping before him. "You are pale. You are not ill, are you, Coventry?"

He was about to tell her he was not ill—or at least to attempt to tell her that—when she touched his forehead. Her hand was ungloved, and for an instant, he knew the fleeting graze of her silken fingertips over his brow.

"You are not feverish," she said, frowning.

He could have argued that he was. But his capacity for

speech was once more frozen. Just as well, for if he could speak, he was afraid he would ask her to touch him again.

"Have I wounded you so gravely with my sharp tongue that you are now refusing to speak to me?" Miss Winter asked next.

Devil take it, she had mentioned her tongue. *Again.*

He could not seem to stop thinking about that deuced troublesome tongue of hers. Or her lips. They were the pink of a wild rose. Bewitching and supple. Too full, really. Tipped upward at the corners, as if she were enjoying a sally at the rest of the world's expense.

And she probably was, the minx.

"I can get you to speak again," she announced, confidence permeating her voice. "Do not look so surprised, Your Grace. I am one of five sisters. You cannot be naïve enough to believe they have not attempted similar tactics against me, and also failed."

He had watched all five Winter sisters closely during the course of this country house party. They were all handfuls, he had no doubt. But the Winter before him was the biggest handful of all. He had seen it clearly from the moment he had first arrived and settled his gaze upon her. Of course his gaze had found her—she was the brightest and the most beautiful of her sisters, with her flaming hair and bold, jewel-toned dresses. The way she swayed her hips, the way she cast her eye upon the company, the way she laughed, the way she danced… It was nothing short of captivating.

She was nothing short of captivating.

And wrong for him as a future duchess.

All wrong.

He needed wealth, not trouble.

She pursed her lips, tilting her head to one side as she considered him. "You have until the count of ten, Your Grace.

At that point, I will have no choice but to use my only means of defense."

Gill moved his mouth without impediment. Cleared his throat. The speechlessness affecting him now was different than his affliction, he realized. He could speak if he wished. But it was Miss Winter and the nearly incapacitating desire he felt for her—misplaced and wrong, but nonetheless present— that was keeping him from speech.

A new phenomenon.

He would have to write this down in his journal later tonight, all the better to examine the pattern. When his head was cleared of the fog currently inhabiting it.

Belatedly, he realized Miss Winter was counting, just as she had warned.

"…seven, eight, nine," she paused for dramatic effect, eying him with raised brows, as if she expected him to flee at any moment.

He did not flee. Instead, he held her stare and his ground both, two feats which were not easy for him when he was in the presence of unfamiliar people.

"Ten!" she announced. "I warned you, Your Grace."

Then, she stepped forward. Nearer still. Her gown billowed around his legs. The feminine scent of her was richer. Notes of jasmine and lily hit him. Her proximity was such that he could see the rich flecks of gold and gray in her blue-green eyes, count the number of freckles upon the dainty bridge of her nose if he wished.

He did not wish.

For in the next breath, she was touching him. Not just touching him. The mad chit had thrust her fingers into his sides and wiggled them about. The action was so unexpected, so shocking, a bark of laughter poured from him. Grinning at him in triumph, she moved her fingers higher, her touch growing firmer.

Belatedly, it occurred to him why he was laughing.

Miss Christabella Winter was tickling him. *Tickling him*, by God.

He caught her wrists, removing her hands from his person, and found his voice at last. "Are you mad, woman?"

"Are *you* mad, Your Grace?" she returned, casting a glance toward his hands, still gripping her wrists.

Strangely, he could not let her go. Her inner wrists were a thing of wonder. Smooth and soft, delicately lined with a tracery of veins, pulsing with the beat of her heart. All of the telltale signs of his affliction were absent. For some reason, Miss Christabella Winter had set him at ease and at sixes and sevens, all at once.

He thought about his response. Some thought him mad. He was well aware of the laughter behind his back, of the stares and whispers, the gossip surrounding him. He was accustomed to scorn and confusion. Gill had never been blessed with his brother's easy charm or his effortless mannerisms.

He was still the boy his father had kept locked in a windowless chamber for twenty hours at a time. Ash did not know about those days. No one did. And Gill had every intention of keeping it that way.

"I am not mad," he told Miss Winter, his voice emerging once more at his bidding. "One might argue otherwise for you, however. You were just tickling me, madam."

But still, he did not release his hold on her. In truth, he liked keeping her where she was. He liked touching her, too. Even if he knew he ought not touch her *or* like it.

"Oh, stuff and nonsense." She rolled her eyes heavenward. "Do not tell me you have never before been tickled."

He gave her his most vexing frown. "I have never before

been tickled."

That gave her pause. Her brow furrowed and her nose scrunched up in adorable fashion. *Strike that.* Nothing about this woman was adorable. She was irritating, he reminded himself. Intolerably forward.

"You have never been tickled," she repeated, her voice dubious, as if she did not believe him.

"Of course not," he clipped, irritated with her. Irritated with himself as well.

He had already decided this woman was not for him. Why did he linger? Why did he engage in conversation? Why could he not let go of her wrists?

"Not even once?" she persisted.

"Not once, Miss Winter," he pronounced, keeping his voice grim. "*Ever.*"

"Well," she said with a sniff and a little huff, as if *she* were aggrieved with *him*, "tickling is the best means of making a sister speak when she is treating you to silence. It works every time. Much like pepper on the pillow of someone you wish to make sneeze."

"I am not your sister, madam," he said, which he was certain could not be more obvious.

For one, he was a man, *blast her*. For another, he was a duke.

"Of course you are not my sister," she agreed. "You are too tall to be any of them. And you do not smell like them, either."

He made a strangled sound. "What *do* I smell like, Miss Winter?"

Posing the question was a mistake. He realized it the moment the last word left his lips. He knew it when she leaned into him, so close, he could bury his face in the fragrant upsweep of her hair if he wished. *Good God*, there were tiny rosebuds woven into the intertwined locks. They were pink, and they matched her lips. And her nose was nearly touching his neck as she inhaled deeply.

"Shaving soap," she decreed, her warm breath puffing over the sensitive slice of neck just above his cravat. "And lemon, with a hint of..." Here she paused, inhaling again. "Musk."

First Miss Christabella Winter had tickled him, and now she was smelling him. Worse, he was imagining those rose-pink lips of hers pressed to his skin, finding their way to his jaw, and thereafter, his mouth.

He swallowed. Hard. "Your nose appears to be function-ing quite well."

"Good," she said.

The lone word confused him. Possibly because her breasts were brushing against his chest.

"Good?" he asked, trying to maintain his calm.

"Yes," she murmured. "You smell delightfully good."

Curse it.

He could say the same of her.

But what would be the use? This bold, unconventional woman was not meant to be his duchess. He required a quiet wife. The sort who would not ask him questions. Or tempt him. Or tickle him. Or invade his person like an enemy army at the portcullis. He preferred solitude. Quiet. Without question, the woman currently sniffing his neck would provide him none of the things he required in a wife.

Except for a massive amount of wealth.

But wealth could be found elsewhere, he reminded him-self sternly.

"This is deuced improper, Miss Winter," he forced him-self to say. "If anyone were to walk into this chamber now, they would think we had been..."

He could not bring himself to form the words. For he feared that if he said them, he would be tempted to bring the words to life.

"Kissing?" she finished for him, because the vixen had no shame.

"No chance of that," he scoffed tightly, far too aware of her face still all but buried in his neck. "I have never engaged in such recklessness before, and I would not begin now with you."

Her head shot back, that bright, blue-green burning into his. "Did you just say you have never kissed a lady before?"

Bloody hell.

His ears were hot. And his cheeks. "I said nothing of the sort. You misunderstood me."

"No." She shook her head slowly, her gaze dipping to his mouth. "I did not. You said you had never kissed before. I fear it is too late to convince me otherwise, Your Grace. The words have already been spoken."

Yes, they had, had they not? And for a man who spoke so little, he had certainly done the devil's own work in revealing that which he had never before admitted aloud. Oh, his brother Ash assumed, and Gill had not made an effort to change that. But he had never before told another soul he had never even kissed a lady.

Nor a mistress.

Nor anyone.

He was a man fully grown, who had never kissed or made love to a woman. And while his brother's rakish ways had more than made up for Gill's lapses, that knowledge was cold comfort. A man was expected to have experience. Carnal knowledge. *By God*, a man was expected to speak to a lady. To woo her. None of which were feats he had ever been able to manage, thanks to his affliction.

The reminders of his failures had him releasing her wrists at last and taking a step back. He had allowed himself to linger far too long in her presence. Somehow, she had made her way past all his defenses. But now, she was once more his enemy. And he could not afford to allow her to storm his battlements.

"Believe what you will, Miss Winter," he forced himself to say before sketching a perfunctory bow. "Good evening to you."

He congratulated himself on striding past her, and leaving the chamber with his head held high, despite his foolish revelation.

But her mocking voice followed him out the door.

"It is only afternoon, Your Grace."

Fuck.

So it was.

Chapter Two

CHRISTABELLA COULD NOT stop thinking about the Duke of Coventry. During dinner the evening before, she had not been able to keep her eyes from him as he dined. Twice, his eyes had made their way to hers. Each time, the connection of their gazes had been shocking. Rather in the way a lightning bolt across the sky was. She felt as if their connection was visceral and real, a shared understanding passing between the two of them.

But he had only looked at her twice.

Twice.

And he had been rather rude in the salon the day before. True, she had been most forward and improper, but he could have handled her lapses with grace. Indeed, she had been quite the fool for him, sniffing him, telling him he smelled good, all but kissing his neck…his strong, deliciously corded, wonderfully masculine neck. The knot in his cravat had been elaborate and tied rather tightly. The prominence of his Adam's apple just above the linen had seemed a temptation she could not resist.

Oh, how she had wanted to press her lips there. To kiss her way higher. All the way to his forbidding mouth. If she had to describe the Duke of Coventry's lips in one word, it would be *grim*. But Christabella had never seen a challenge without wanting to conquer it. Or, in this instance, conquer *him.* His lips, specifically.

She wanted to kiss him.

To be his first kiss.

Oh, dear. Her preoccupation was beginning to become a problem.

"Christabella," said her eldest sister Pru, cutting through her thoughts. "Where is your mind wandering to now?"

To delicious, tempting, entirely wicked thoughts.

As usual.

She grinned at Pru, unashamed. "Wandering near and far, as always."

"To thoughts of the book," her sister Eugie guessed.

As was their customary habit, the five Winter sisters had descended upon a single chamber to prepare themselves for the afternoon's drawing room festivities. In this instance, they had settled upon Pru's for their tête-à-tête.

"There is nothing wrong with *The Tale of Love*," she told Eugie, giving her sister a forbidding frown as she sank her earbobs into place. "Reading it has proven most enlightening. For all of us, I daresay."

Pink cheeks and guilty silences met her words.

Just as she had supposed.

"I only glanced at it," offered Bea, the youngest, by way of explanation.

"Yes," Christabella reminded her sister, "but you have gone and fallen in love with Mr. Hart, and as the two of you have been looking quite cozy recently, I doubt you even have need of the book."

Bea's cheeks deepened to a guiltier shade of scarlet. It was no secret she and their brother's right-hand man, Merrick Hart, were wildly in love. But her chin tipped up in a show of defiance anyway.

"I have no notion what you are speaking about, Christabella," her youngest sister said. "Have you been reading more of those silly books?"

"There is nothing silly about the books I read," she informed Bea. "There is, however, something very telling in the color of your cheeks. Your hair was quite mussed the other day when I saw you leaving one of the salons. Mr. Hart was not far behind you."

"It is wicked of you to suggest anything untoward occurred," Bea said, but she was blushing even more.

Christabella grinned. "I approve, of course. You must know that, dearest. You and Mr. Hart make a delightful couple, and the two of you are so in love, I am quite envious."

"You do make a beautiful couple," Eugie agreed.

"Disgustingly so," added Grace, the most pragmatic of all the sisters.

"*Wonderfully* so," corrected Pru, the eldest of them all, and the de facto leader of their coterie.

Grace grumbled something about love seeming to be a pestilence.

"How can you think of love in such cruel terms when you are being wooed by a rake?" Christabella asked her sister.

She was curious. Grace had the handsome rakehell, Viscount Aylesford, chasing after her. *If only*, sighed a voice inside Christabella. There was nothing more delicious than a beautiful man with a bad reputation, as far as she was concerned. To have one interested in her would be delightfully wicked.

"I am not being wooed by him," Grace reminded her. "He has settled upon me as his feigned betrothed, and he has stolen our book to do it."

"That particular volume is one of my favorites," she allowed, "but I trust you will find the means of seeing it restored to me."

"One way or another," Grace said grimly.

"Enough of that," Eugie interjected. "I am missing an earbob. Do you see it?"

Christabella and her other sisters exchanged knowing looks. Eugie had been distinctly disheveled upon her arrival at Pru's chamber. And flushed. And breathless. The Winter sisters had all seemed to be getting into mischief this Christmastide—Christabella the exception, of course.

Her lack of success at finding a rake to kiss her prodded Christabella into action.

"I am certain you did not lose it during an assignation with Lord Hertford," she said drily.

Eugie was promised to the earl, who was more familiarly known by the sobriquet the Prince of Proper. Not a rake, to be sure, but still. It seemed to Christabella that all her sisters were losing their hearts to the gentlemen around them.

Meanwhile, Christabella could not even find a gentleman to flirt with her. The Duke of Coventry had refused to speak for much of their time alone together.

"I did not have an assignation," Eugie denied.

The tone of her voice, however, gave her away.

"Sisters," Pru chastised. "Christabella, we must not forget we are one another's greatest allies. Reviled though we may be, the Winter family stands together."

"Of course we do," Christabella acknowledged, smoothing some stray wisps of her wayward hair into place before Pru's looking glass. "We are Winters first."

Though their family was notoriously unaccepted by most of the members of the peerage—unless they required the Winter family coin, naturally—they were a proud and fierce lot. They loved each other mightily. Their loyalty was to one another. With so much change happening around her—her brother wedded, many of her sisters on the threshold of marriage—Christabella could only hope they would always remain so.

"No matter where we go, or who we become," Pru added, "we will always be Winters."

"Though our names may change, our hearts will remain forever constant," Bea added.

Christabella turned away from the glass, allowing her gaze to sweep over all her sisters. How she loved them. They were each so very different, and yet so much a part of the fabric of their family. Through everything they had endured, the six Winter siblings had always been the sternest supporters of one another. For so long, they had been all they had. And they had made their little family work.

But it could not remain as it was forever.

Change was on the horizon.

For all of them.

And, Christabella dared hope, herself.

Why she thought of the stern, forbidding countenance of the Duke of Coventry then, she could not say. Kissing him would be lovely. But he was not the man she was meant to spend the rest of her life with, she reminded herself sternly. She wanted a rake, not a man who was cool and quiet and rude. Certainly not a man who had no experience kissing a lady.

But she would enjoy teaching him how to kiss, she decided with a secretive smile.

Oh, yes she would. And she would learn precisely what she needed to do to woo a man herself along the way.

GILL HAD GROWN bored of every drawing room entertainment that had thus far been invented, he was sure of it. This one was no different than the rest. He stood on the periphery of the assemblage, watching them engaged in charades. Again.

Another three slow strides to his left, and the door leading to freedom was almost within reach. As a man who could not bear much society at all, he had become adroit at removing himself from situations he found displeasing without anyone else being the wiser. There was an art, he had discovered, to fleeing a chamber. Initially, he had left every gathering to which he had been invited, struck by the loudness of the sounds, the brightness of the lights, the heat, the chatter, the eyes upon him...

It had all been far, far too much for him to bear. But over time, Gill had settled upon a way he could flee without being overly conspicuous in his departure. It left his host and hostess more at ease, and it severely reduced the number of whispers surrounding him. All he needed to do was take incremental steps to the door. No one noticed. Eventually, he was near enough to cross the threshold into glorious freedom.

He stopped, pretending to watch Miss Bea Winter demonstrating what appeared to be a farmer pitching hay. And then, as the company began shouting their guesses, he took three more steps. As the guesses continued, he took two more. The doorway called to him like a beacon from a lighthouse on shore.

His cravat was too tight. His palms practically teemed with perspiration. And that dreaded tightness in his chest had returned, the one that made him feel as if he could scarcely breathe. He needed to leave.

The company continued guessing. Miss Bea Winter made further efforts to demonstrate the unfortunate task she had selected. From this angle, it rather appeared as if she were now baking a pie. Gill did not give a damn what she was attempting to mimic. All he wanted was escape.

Another step. Then another. Someone shouted a loud guess that she had been plucking a Michaelmas goose. The merrymakers laughed. Gill pressed his advantage. Three more steps, and he was out the door, over the threshold, his strides taking him down the hall where blissful silence reigned.

"Your Grace?"

What the devil? He stopped, mid-stride, and pivoted on his heel, certain he would not find anyone there. Certain he had imagined the voice. Certain no one would have taken note of his stealthy flight from charades.

But there stood the woman who had been haunting his thoughts ever since the day before. Her hair was as brazen as she was, and every bit as delectable. Stray tendrils of brilliant, red curls had broken free of her coiffure, no doubt in her earlier depiction of an irate heifer. Somehow, she had managed to make even the bovine seem seductive. He had watched her in a combination of consternation and lust, overwhelmed by his reaction to her.

In truth, she was part of the reason why he was retreating from charades.

He stared at her, resenting her.

Wanting her.

"Your Grace, is something amiss?" she elaborated, striding forward with an expression of pure concern. "I noticed you leaving while the game is still carrying on, and you did an excellent job of guessing when it was my turn…"

That was because he could not take his eyes from her. Because she was all he saw, like it or not. Because he longed for her. Desperately. And he damned well knew he ought not. Longed for her so bloody much that his voice had emerged from him earlier.

Rusty, it was true. More of a croak than a bark. But he had *spoken*, in the midst of a silly drawing room game, surrounded by others. And he had not felt the choking burn of bile. Perhaps that was because she had met and held his gaze, seemingly cheering him on with her bright eyes and grin of unadulterated delight. He had fallen headlong into her, forgetting the others. A mistake, of course.

Just thinking about the crush of revelers within Abingdon House's tremendous drawing room was enough to make his chest tight. He cleared his throat. But no words would emerge now. *Damnation*, this was a fine time for his affliction to strike. Strangely, although his throat had seized, his cock was not similarly afflicted. It was raging and hard. Instantly. Pressed to the fall of his breeches.

"Coventry?" She moved nearer to him in the hall.

There was not much chance of them being caught, with the door to the drawing room closed once more and no one else having yet emerged. But at any moment, a servant could come upon them. They were risking a great deal by lingering here, unchaperoned.

He could smell her sweet scent. Summer blossoms and divine, seductive woman. Wicked, altogether wrong, Christabella Winter.

He found his voice at last.

"Why are you following me?" he demanded. Not precisely what he had meant to say.

She stopped, then pinned him with a ferocious frown. "I was concerned about you, Your Grace. You appeared pale when you left the chamber. Almost as if you were about to retch, in fact…"

"You have gall, madam," he bit out. Defensively, yes. Because it was bad enough he could not conduct himself in the company of others. When anyone had the temerity to remind him of his weakness, it made him livid.

"I have honesty," she dared to correct him. "And a wayward tongue, it is true. One of my weaknesses, I suppose. I have never known when to keep quiet and when I ought to speak. As a result, I simply speak whenever I wish."

Of course she did, the vexing creature.

She also had to cease saying the word *tongue* in his presence.

Every instinct within him screamed to close the distance between them and haul her into his arms. What he would do with her after that, he had no notion. Because he was a virgin. A stupid, terrified virgin.

His brother had bedded half the ladies of London, and he, the duke, had not even managed to press his lips to the mouth of one. Not for lack of Ash's attempts on his behalf.

"Your Grace." Suddenly, there was a hand on his arm, gentle and yet strong. He was being led to a door as the scent of summer blooms filled his senses.

He allowed it. His legs were moving. His heart was pounding. The affliction threatened to overwhelm him, but he forced himself to combat it as he had learned. Long, slow breaths. Closing his mind as if it were a door.

When his mind opened, he was closeted within a chamber, alone with Miss Christabella Winter. With her hands upon him. Her head was tilted back, her countenance concerned, her lips parted. She stroked his biceps, the place where he had built muscle through rigid labor at his country estate. He had worked alongside his tenants for the last summer, attempting to find his way.

Laboring suited him. He was not meant to be a duke, he had always feared, and yet, the title, the vast lands and all its inhabitants, and his father's colossal debts remained his burdens to bear.

"No one will intrude upon us here," Miss Winter reassured him as her hands caressed. "What is the matter, Your

Grace?"

He was what was the matter. Or rather, his mind was. His blasted affliction. He had suffered it for as long as he could recall, beginning back to the days when his father had kept him locked within that damned chamber.

But he could not say that. Not to this brazen female continuing to make herself far too familiar with his person.

"You are the matter, Miss Winter," he snapped, irritated with himself for his weakness.

Irritated with *her* for his unwanted reaction to her.

She stiffened as if he had slapped her, taking a step back and removing her touch. "Forgive me, Your Grace. I often forget myself. I meant no insult."

Yet, she had insulted him by trundling him into this bloody salon as if he needed to hide himself away like a shameful secret. Because he *was* a shameful secret, and that was what smarted most.

The Duke of Coventry could not even remain in a drawing room for a meaningless game of charades without turning into a Bedlamite.

"You should not be alone with me, unchaperoned," he said, all he could manage.

Perspiration filmed his upper lip. His heart yet pounded. But there was one undeniable reaction to her: his prick was as hard as it had ever been. Even in such a state, his body knew what it wanted, and it wanted hers.

"Of course I should not," she agreed, giving him a look he imagined she might also use upon someone who had just kicked a puppy. "But I was thinking of your welfare, Your Grace. You seemed...ill."

Ill, yes.

That was one word for it.

Of all the frustrations in Gill's life, here was the greatest one: that he had no control over his own mind or body. None. A part of him had hoped, futilely, that he would somehow outgrow his affliction. Or that he would be strong enough to conquer it. But his affliction was not about strength, and he had been forced to acknowledge that truth, regardless of how daunting he found it.

"I am," he began, only to pause, struggling to find a suitable explanation. "I do not prefer gatherings of people. Or speaking. I find silence far more comforting."

"Silence," she repeated, blinking, as though the word was unfamiliar.

When a lady chattered as much as she did, he supposed it would be an unfamiliar word.

"Silence, yes." He swallowed, then inhaled, trying to regain domination of his senses. His heart seemed quite unwilling to obey. "Quiet is peaceful and comforting."

Though in truth, he did not particularly enjoy silence either. Silence reminded him of the chamber. The darkness. The stale air. The helplessness.

Silence gave him nightmares.

Speaking robbed his voice.

What a hopeless muddle he was.

"Complete silence?" Miss Winter wanted to know. "What of the birds singing in spring? Do you like that sound?"

He pondered her query, never having thought about birds before. "Yes, I suppose."

"Or the wind rustling through the trees," she added. "Do you find fault with that sound, Your Grace?"

He cleared his throat again. "I cannot recall finding fault with it."

"How about the waves crashing upon the shore?" she asked next. "My brother took us all to Brighton once, and it was quite beautiful, even though there was a storm churning off shore. Indeed, the storm almost made it more exquisite, if I think upon it now. We often forget how powerful the world around us is, just how much we are at its mercy."

She was strikingly astute for a chit with a wayward tongue.

Against his will, Gill was beginning to like Miss Christabella Winter.

"I do not object to the sound of the sea," he told her grudgingly. "Indeed, it is quite calming, in the proper circumstances."

"What about the sound of a mewling kitten?" she ventured next. "Or the bark of a sweet little puppy? Do you like the sound of the pianoforte? The jangling of tack? One of my favorite sounds is that of a stream, gently rushing, never stopping. There is something so magnificent about water, I find. Do you not find it so?"

"Magnificent, yes," he agreed.

But he was staring at her. Taking her in. He was not thinking about water at all. Rather, he was noting the precise shade of her hair, the tints of gold within it. Noting the copper, the way it almost seemed like a flame, the hues all dancing together in the sunlight. And then, he was looking at her long lashes, her blue-green eyes, her wide lips, her creamy throat, her perfect bosom...

Fucking hell, this was no good.

No good at all.

"Then you *do* like sounds," she pronounced, as if she had just solved some great mystery. "But you do not prefer conversation. That is the sound to which you object, is it not?"

She was right, confound her.

"I converse when I must," he defended himself.

That was a lie, and he knew it. For he often eschewed

speaking altogether. Or he allowed Ash to speak for him. Ash, with his smooth, rakish ways, spoke effortlessly. Gill, weighed down by his affliction, was abysmal at conducting any sort of meaningful dialogue.

"I thought you did not speak because you are haughty," she confessed then, guileless as ever. "But that is not the way of it. I see that now. You are truly affected by interaction with others. Not by sounds themselves."

Once again, the irritating Miss Christabella Winter was proving far too perceptive.

He shifted his weight from one foot to the other. "Yes."

There. He admitted his weakness, his inability to act as a proper duke ought.

Gill waited for her to recoil. To express her horror. To flee. Worse, to laugh at him.

Instead, she smiled. And, *Lord help him*, it was the most beauteous, genuine, pleasing smile he had ever beheld. It was a smile that burrowed its way into his soul. It was a smile he would never forget. It was a smile to surpass all others which would come after it.

"Oh, how fortunate, Your Grace," she told him, that bewitching smile of hers deepening. "I know just the remedy for your ailments."

"You do?" he was skeptical. Because no woman had ever spoken to him this much. He inevitably seemed to scare them away.

"Yes." She tilted her head, her gaze one with his. "Me."

Chapter Three

"*Y*OU?"

The Duke of Coventry's voice was incredulous. And icy. Indeed, it echoed in the chamber as if it had been a shot fired from a pistol.

Her courage flagged.

Perhaps she had been wrong after all.

But, no. She would not retreat. She had already come too far.

"Yes," she said, tipping her chin in defiance, daring him to naysay her. "Me. I am the remedy for your ailments. Not that I wish to brag, but I would be remiss if I failed to mention that I have now calmed you into speaking with me on nothing short of two separate occasions."

Which, of course, she had.

And, naturally, she wanted to know why.

But also, she had already settled upon her brilliant notion of teaching the Duke of Coventry to kiss. The two of them could practice together. And then, he could garner the courage to woo another lady of his choosing, and she could go on to practice her wiles upon a deserving rake.

There were only two small problems with her plan. One: she was no longer certain lack of experience was the duke's only romantic impediment. Two: she was no longer certain she could kiss the Duke of Coventry and then blissfully encourage him to court another woman. Not now when she stood in such proximity to him, she practically felt his presence like a spark skittering over her.

But she would worry about these problems later. Perhaps. For the moment, Coventry's delicious blue gaze was firmly fixed upon her, and she was soaking up his attention as if she were drought-ridden soil and he were the rain.

"You have vexed me into speaking," he said. His tone was cutting.

She ignored the sting. "Have I vexed you, Your Grace? Specify how, if you please, so I may remedy my future comportment."

He pursed his lips. And *heavens*, how fine his lips were.

Perfectly sculpted, a delicious shade of pink. She wondered if they would feel as firm against her mouth as they appeared, or if they would be soft and lush. If they would give…

"You have been far too familiar," said those luscious lips.

Oh.

Yes, she supposed she had. But she had never cared much for rules. Polite society was silly, as far as she was concerned. If there existed a book she was not allowed to read, she wanted to read it. If there was a word she was forbidden from speaking, she wanted to shout it. If there was a man she was not allowed to kiss, well, she wanted to kiss him.

Of course she did.

Especially if the man in question was the Duke of Coventry.

"I should beg your pardon," she said, knowing it was what was expected of her.

"You *should*, or you *do*?" he asked pointedly.

"I should," she responded, just to needle him.

"You are not sorry, then," the duke observed, his tone as

forbidding as his countenance.

She wondered if he had ever known a carefree day in his life. She also wondered why the supposition he had not should bother her so. Certainly, the duke had never shown her a kindness or a mercy. Nor had he given her any indication he enjoyed her company. Quite the opposite, in fact.

"I know what is expected of me," she said, her tone challenging. "You *think* I should beg your pardon, Your Grace. Society has its whims and its rules, and we are all expected to follow them without question. But if I have indeed been familiar with you, I do not regret it. This is the most entertainment I have enjoyed since my arrival here in Oxfordshire."

That was the truth, all of it. She thrived upon gaiety and interesting characters, parties and routs and balls, the whirl and bustle of London life. The country had been remarkably staid thus far, with all the rakehells in attendance otherwise occupied by her sisters. Merriment and games grew old. The Duke of Coventry, however, presented a challenge.

Christabella Winter adored challenges.

And handsome men.

Not necessarily in that order.

The Duke of Coventry sighed. "In truth, your lack of propriety is somehow charming. And disarming as well. I suspect that is quite intentional. You strike me as the sort who could lead an army into battle with ease."

"Ah, but I would never lead an army into battle," she told him. "I would convince them all the cause was futile and they should return to their homes to live happily ever after."

"And then their villages would be pillaged and burned, they would be murdered in their sleep, and the enemy would overtake their land, their wives, and homes," he countered, quite brutally.

She blinked.

An unexpected darkness lurked behind his quiet façade. What had happened to the Duke of Coventry in his life to render him so embittered?

She wanted to know, and yet, a part of her did not.

Christabella frowned at him. "That is a harsh interpretation, Your Grace."

"That is an *accurate* interpretation, Miss Winter," he said, a stubborn note entering his baritone.

They were engaging in an argument.

Her frown turned into a grin. She felt as if she had won. Because he was speaking to her, nevertheless. He had not frozen, and the haunted expression had fled.

"I believe you have just proven me correct, Your Grace." Energy and delight suddenly filled her. She had to move. And there was only one way she could conceive of doing so. She closed the distance between them once more.

Scant distance.

He smelled delicious, of lemons and bay and shaving soap.

She wanted to touch him again. Her fingers almost itched with the need. His muscles had been so...strong.

"How have I proven you correct?" he asked.

The husky rumble of his voice was as delectable as his scent.

"You are still speaking with me," she said, her gaze dipping once more to his forbidding mouth. "Quite eloquently, even if somewhat rudely. I have settled upon an excellent plan. Would you like to hear it now?"

"No," he said.

The disagreeable man.

She gave him a quelling look. "I am going to tell you anyway."

"I never doubted it," he grumbled, scrubbing a hand along his jaw.

But he did not go. She took it as a sign of his acquiescence.

"I am going to kiss you," she pronounced.

GILL HAD MISHEARD the maddening creature.

Surely, he had.

For there was no other explanation to describe the words he thought he had just heard her utter. Individually, they meant nothing at all. Strung together, one sentence of six little words, they proved his undoing.

"You," he sputtered, then stopped.

Because he was not certain if his tongue would properly function. Or that his breeches could survive the painful surge of his cockstand.

"Me," she said brightly, her tone agreeable.

As if they had been speaking about a triviality such as the newly fallen snow, or the unseasonable cold. As if they exchanged pleasantries in a drawing room. As if she had not just spoken the sentence that had set him aflame.

"Miss Winter," he began, "surely I misheard you. You could not have said what I thought you just uttered..."

"Of course I could have." She smiled at him yet again, sending prickles down his spine. "And I did."

Her boldness should be aggrieving. Shocking. Instead, he found it entrancing. Intoxicating. Perhaps because all the blood in his body had rushed to a singular portion of his anatomy.

Because she had stepped even nearer. Her gown—white satin with an ivory lace overlay—fluttered into him. Her hands settled upon his shoulders. Her face—utterly lovely—tipped back. Her blue-green eyes seared him. Her mouth was a sinful promise he could not deny.

Yes, he could, he told himself. He was stronger than seduction. He could withstand her greatest efforts.

He had never kissed a lady before.

He would not begin with this flighty Winter chit, who followed him about and touched him as if it were her right. Who announced she was going to kiss him with such cool calm. Who was bold and daring, with her blazing hair, her sharp tongue, and her maddeningly divine scent of summer blooms.

"Miss Winter, you cannot simply go about kissing the gentlemen in the house party," he told her.

But the words lacked the sting they should possess, and he knew it. And one of his hands had settled upon her waist whilst the other had found its way to her shoulder. He was touching her, *by God*. Without the affliction setting in as it had on previous occasions. His heart did not pound. His skin did not perspire.

Impossible.

She was warm, heating his skin through all the layers of fabric keeping him from her flesh. And soft, so bloody soft.

"I do not want to go about kissing all the gentleman," she said softly. Sweetly. "I only want to kiss you."

Her cheeks turned pink as she said the last.

It was the first sign this wild Winter was capable of experiencing embarrassment. She was so forward and bold, where he was quiet and contained. He was a breeze whispering through a vast forest, and she was a maelstrom overwhelming the coast.

Somehow, he found that intriguing. He found *her* intriguing.

His own gaze slipped to her lips. They were full and pouty, inviting and wicked. Everything a woman's mouth should be.

He swallowed. "You want to kiss me."

"Yes," she said.

"Only me," he clarified.

As if that mattered. The voice inside him was strident and demanding. *Kiss her*, it said. *Take her mouth with yours.* He had already forgotten his stern inner admonition to kiss only the woman he would wed. All he could think about was the way this woman's lips would feel beneath his. Would they be soft and supple? What would happen after their mouths met? He had read a great deal on the subject in an effort to better prepare himself for the inevitable bedding he would need to do with his duchess.

Yet, as he drank in the sight of Miss Christabella Winter, and as he felt her so vital and luscious in his arms, he could think of nothing but her.

"Only you," she said then. "If you wish it, of course. I thought it would help us both, you see."

"Help us?" Somehow, his hand was traveling up and down her spine, stroking her. Bringing her closer. "How?"

"We shall both of us be the better for our practice." She grinned.

Her hands remained on his shoulders, resting there. He liked the weight of them, so small and dainty. Liked the way her face tipped back to accommodate for his greater height. Liked those delicious freckles on her nose. Liked her proposal. These kisses she suggested.

"Practice," he repeated, turning the word over in his mind.

It made sense. If he were able to properly kiss a woman, perhaps he would fare better in his mad quest to obtain a wealthy wife. How was he to compete with charming rakehells like his brother if he could neither speak to a lady nor show her his intent in other fashions? Ash said the fairer sex adored kissing. *Everywhere*, the rascal had said, grinning triumphantly.

Somehow, he thought of kissing Miss Winter. Everywhere. From the tip of her nose, to her sweet lips, to her smooth throat, all the way to her full breasts until he found his way to his knees, and from there he would lift her skirts and press his face between her thighs...

Curse it, such thoughts were ill becoming, and he knew it.

Gill was not ignorant of what passed between a man and a woman. He was merely incapable of performing it. His brother had brought London's most famed courtesan to him, and still, the affliction had returned, striking with a vengeance. The memory served as a bitter reminder that even if he now held Miss Winter in his arms and the notion of practicing kisses with her beckoned like the beacon of a lighthouse to a ship in distress off shore, the affliction could seize him at any second.

Rendering kisses and practice and everything else impossible.

"Practice," Miss Winter was saying now, her bright gaze firmly on his lips. Her voice was a seductive rasp. "Yes, we shall be a boon for one another. It is the perfect plan."

He could not think of a more *imperfect* plan.

Gentlemen did not practice kissing ladies they had no intention of wedding. *Devil take it*, they did not practice kissing ladies at all. Only scoundrels did, and that was so they could find their way beneath said ladies' skirts.

Gill needed to find a proper, wealthy bride.

He needed to turn his mind to accomplishing his task before the estates went into further ruin.

But Christabella Winter's eyes were burning into his once more. And she was a decadent temptation in his arms. He could still speak, breathe, and move. It was rather a miracle, of sorts. Or perhaps she was. A temptation, for certain.

What would be the harm? asked that damned voice inside him.

One kiss.

That is all.

Or perhaps two. Three? Mayhap even four...

"Very well," he found himself saying. "One kiss. For practice, you understand. Nothing more."

She beamed.

His inner sense of caution returned like a smack to the face. "And pray, do not think to entrap me into marriage with kisses, Miss Winter. It will not happen."

Her lips twitched, almost as if she were suppressing laughter. "You have no fear on that score, Your Grace. I am marrying a rake. Hence, the necessity of practice. I should hate to disappoint my future husband with the kisses of a tyro."

Here, now. She was betrothed? That was certainly news. He had heard nothing of the sort.

Even so, something inside him was irreparably broken. Because the knowledge did nothing to relieve the uncomfortable state of his cock as it ought.

"I cannot think your husband would approve of you kissing another gentleman, even if he did not appreciate a neophyte," he told her, giving her a frown.

Truly, the chit was incorrigible.

"Fortunately, he shall never know," she said, confirming his deduction. "That is the beauty of kissing practice. It is *practice*. For both of us. Just as my future husband will have no notion I ever learned how to kiss with the Duke of

35

Coventry, your future wife will have no inkling your first kiss was with one of the wicked Winters."

Kissing practice.

His cock twitched.

His inner sense of right and wrong, however, would not be seduced. "You are betraying your betrothed, Miss Winter."

"I do not yet have a betrothed." She smiled. "You see? My plan is flawless."

She was flawless.

Thank Christ she did not already have a betrothed.

The notion had been enough to make him feel itchy. And angry. And jealous.

Irrationally so.

He struggled to follow her logic. "You said you are marrying a rake, Miss Winter. What else was I to surmise from such a statement?"

"Oh, I am," she said, her smile deepening to reveal a lone groove in her left cheek. "However, I have yet to meet him. There is no better time than now to perfect my kissing skills. I shall need them, of course. I would hate to think my husband found my kisses regrettable and untutored."

He almost choked. First, that dimple. *Good God*, that fucking dimple. Second, no one would ever find the kisses of Miss Christabella Winter regrettable and untutored. He was bloody well certain of it.

No betrothed, taunted the voice.

Kissing practice. What sort of female arrived at such a nonsensical notion? And why could he not seem to send her from his arms?

"Very well," he found himself saying. "But just this once, Miss Winter. Never again after this sole occasion."

"You will not regret it, Your Grace," she said, still smiling like the Bedlamite she undoubtedly was. Still beautiful, damn it. She caressed his cheek then, just fleetingly, before stepping out of his embrace. "Our practice will commence tomorrow."

"Tomorrow?" The word was torn from him, a denial. If he was to kiss her, he wanted to kiss her now, *damn it.*

"Yes, tomorrow, Your Grace." She was already halfway across the salon. "We have lingered alone together too long as it is. I dare not remain much longer, for fear we are caught. A forced marriage is the last thing either of us wants, yes? Kissing practice must wait for another day. But, oh, I am so pleased you have seen the wisdom of my plan! I will meet you in the west wing, shall we say, around two o'clock? Far less chance of discovery there."

Everything she said made sense.

Of course it did.

What did not make sense was the ache left behind by the absence of her in his arms.

"I am not certain I will be able to accommodate an assignation," he informed her, feeling churlish at the unaffected manner in which she was flitting away. She had just changed everything inside him and tied him up in veritable knots.

"You will," she said as she reached the door, spinning back to face him. Her tone was confident. Knowing. She looked like a goddess come to life.

One sent to tempt and torment him.

"And how do you know that?" he asked, irritated with her. Irritated with himself as well. He should be able to withstand this beautiful minx.

"Because you want to kiss me, Your Grace," she announced, her smile turning into a rakish grin. "And also because I disarm you. You have just carried on an entire conversation without once turning into an icicle."

He did not turn into an icicle, *by God.*

He opened his mouth to tell her so.

"Yes, you do turn into an icicle," she argued before he could speak. "But a very handsome icicle, Your Grace. You see? You are ice, and I am flame. I melt you. That is why my plan is so perfect. Tomorrow in the red salon, in the west wing, at three o'clock."

She was right. Blast her. Except for the time.

Her back was to him once more when he called out.

"Miss Winter?"

She spun about, her brows raised. "Your Grace?"

"You have the time confused," he growled. "Initially, you said two o'clock. Now you have just said three o'clock. Which is it to be?"

Miss Winter laughed. "You noticed. I hoped you would."

Miss Christabella Winter was trouble. No question.

"Two or three?" he demanded.

"Two," she said, before dipping into a proper curtsy. "Until then, Your Grace."

And then, she vanished over the threshold, the door closing quietly behind her. He stood there, blinking, frozen—like a bloody icicle, it was true—thinking that but for the scent of summer blossoms lingering in the air, she might have been the product of his imagination. He would have been better off had she been, he was sure.

Just as sure as he was that he would be meeting her in the west wing tomorrow at two o'clock. Yes indeed, Miss Christabella was trouble. Capital-T trouble.

And he was capital-I intrigued.

Chapter Four

CHRISTABELLA WAS THE most reckless of all her siblings. This, she knew.

She was also the most romantic at heart. The most idealistic. The dreamer.

This, she also knew.

She relished risks. Rejoiced in rule breaking. Delighted in danger.

Unlike her brother and her sisters, Christabella did not mind being considered a wicked Winter by polite society. She did not long for respectability. Not even a title. All she wanted was a man who kissed her and made her feel as if the earth had shifted beneath her slippers.

Which was why it made complete sense and also no sense at all that she was currently in a minor salon deep within the west wing of Abingdon House, pacing the floor and awaiting the Duke of Coventry. First, the man was not a rake. He had never even kissed another.

Scowling at the mantel clock, she turned on her heel to perform another circumnavigation of the chamber. It was a quarter past two, and the duke was nowhere to be found. Nary even the drop of a footfall in the hall, not a creak. Not a note slipped to her surreptitiously. Nothing.

No word.

No duke.

It was just as well, she told herself with a sigh. There was no reason why she should be aggrieved that Coventry had chosen not to meet with her. If he did not want to kiss a lady, that was his problem, not hers. She could very easily find a replacement, she was certain. For now that she had settled upon the plan of learning how to kiss before she met her husband, she could not let it go.

True, the only man she could conceive herself wishing to kiss at the moment was the maddening duke. And true, her heart still beat faster when she thought of him. Also true, thoughts of his mouth had kept her up all night, into the wee hours of dawn. She had contemplated how she should kiss him first. Or if she should allow him. If she should kiss him slowly or quickly, if she should engage her tongue as the characters in *The Tale of Love* did.

And she had touched herself.

Yes, she had.

Her fingers had found her most sensitive place. But this time, she had imagined it was Coventry's long, elegant fingers stroking her. Stroking her as he kissed her…

"Oh my," she muttered to herself as she paced the chamber once more. Her body was heated. All too aware. The ache between her thighs could not be answered. Not here.

And all for a man who had not summoned the courage to seek her out.

Why, the next time she was alone with him, she would box his handsome ears for—

The door to the chamber opened.

She spun around.

There he stood. Tall. Golden. Leonine. Unsure of himself. The door closed at his back, and he remained where he was. His gaze found hers, unerringly, even across the chamber.

He bowed.

Quite elegantly, too. She could find no fault in it.

She curtseyed, thinking it silly to observe the proprieties when they were meeting in secret. And yet, thinking how it seemed to heighten the anticipation, until the air between them was fairly quivering with a mixture of formality and anticipation.

Wicked anticipation.

"Miss Winter," he said.

"You are late," she told him. "*Your Grace.*"

She was mocking him. She knew she ought not, but she had just spent one quarter of an hour believing he would not deign to meet her. Worse, that he would not deign to kiss her. He had earned some nettling.

"I am sorry." He moved toward her, his strides slow and deliberate.

For a man who was not at all a rake, he certainly made her heart beat faster.

She watched him approach, and she could not help but think about kissing him. But she was determined not to give in so easily.

"Why were you late?" she asked.

He stopped before her, just out of reach, his blue eyes hot and intense upon hers. He said nothing. His jaw was rigid. She understood he was struggling. Battling against whatever internal forces made him detest conversation. She had taken note that her initial interactions with him always began in a more stilted fashion. He was the icicle. She was the fire.

Which meant she would need to take the reins of this particular moment.

She took two steps, then settled her hands upon his shoulders. They were rigid. Strong. He did not possess the lean build of a rake or a lord. Rather, he was sturdy and thick, much like a laborer.

She liked it.

She liked *him*.

"Your Grace?" she prompted, making certain their eyes remained locked. "If you do not tell me why you were late, I shall have to guess."

He made a low sound in his throat, part growl.

A promising sign.

"You forgot how to read the time?" she asked. "You were waylaid by a dragon en route to the west wing? You had to rescue a mouse from a hungry feline?"

He made another sound.

"Oh," she continued airily, as though he had spoken, "you need not tell me dragons are not real. But being delayed by a mythical creature is one of the only acceptable reasons for your tardiness. Obviously, rescuing a mouse would be an excellent excuse, for mice are quite adorable. Mouse ears are endearing, do you not think? And their noses. To say nothing of those tiny paws…"

"Miss Winter," he said at last, his voice sounding choked.

She tried not to smile. "Yes, Your Grace?"

"You are the strangest creature I have ever met."

Hmm. Not precisely the words of a practiced seducer. He would have to work upon that.

"I am neither strange, nor a creature," she informed him, allowing her gaze to travel over the rest of his handsome countenance now that it seemed she had managed to thaw some of his ice.

His jaw was so wide and strong. She could not contain the urge to touch it. So she gave in, gently running her fingers over the delicious angle. His face appeared smoothly shaven, but there was the slightest hint of his whiskers abrading her fingertips.

He inhaled swiftly, his lips parting. "You were just attempting to convince me a rodent is adorable, and now you are petting me, Miss Winter."

She had to stifle her laughter at his bewildered tone. "Have you ever seen a mouse, Your Grace?"

His jaw tensed beneath her touch. "Of course not. Nor have I any wish to."

"If you saw one, you would know how right I am," she whispered, stroking his jaw again. "And I am not petting you at all. I am caressing you. Shall I stop?"

He swallowed. "No."

Ah, His Grace approved.

Excellent, because so did she. Touching him was making the ache between her thighs blossom and grow. It was also making her nipples tighten into hard little buds beneath her stays. His citrus and bay scent, coupled with his nearness, were doing strange things to her senses.

"Shall we use our tongues when we kiss?" she asked him next.

She had been pondering the question in preparation of their meeting.

"Miss Winter," he bit out.

She had shocked him, she supposed. "Apparently the use of tongues can be quite delightful. Tongues are wet, of course. It does seem an odd thing to put one's tongue in the mouth of another. But I am willing to try it if you are."

"You need to stop saying that in my presence," he rasped.

"Stop saying what?" She frowned, trailing her touch down his throat, over his cravat, to rest her hand over his thumping heart.

"Tongue," he clarified succinctly.

And then, he dipped his head and sealed their lips in one quick motion.

HER MOUTH WAS even softer than he had imagined.

That was Gill's first coherent thought.

The second thought was that her breasts crushed against his chest was the purest form of heaven he had ever experienced. Or torment, considering he could do nothing more than hold her in his arms and kiss her.

But that was quickly becoming everything as sensations buffeted him. Her scent teased him: rose and lily of the valley. Her lips were warm. Her body was giving and supple, curving to his as if she were made for him. He cupped her face with his hands, relishing the smoothness of her skin.

He moved his lips over hers, lightly at first, until she made a sweet sound of need, and he lost control. He pressed his mouth harder, and it became apparent that she was right. There was nothing he wanted more than to taste her. His tongue explored as he deepened the kiss instinctively.

All the worries fogging his mind and hindering his actions fell away. He had been fretting over his decision to meet her. Half-convinced he ought to leave her in the salon, awaiting him. To never again find himself alone with the beautifully wild Christabella Winter.

But as he had paced his chamber, the minutes ticking by, he had not been able to stay away. His body, ever having a mind of its own, had reigned supreme, forcing him to the red salon. He had been moved by his need for her as much as his curiosity. Both were overwhelming.

As overwhelming as the sensation of her tongue meeting his. A sudden rush of desire hit him. He wanted to consume her. To kiss her until their mouths ached. To fill her with his cock. All the pent-up lust within him was unleashed. It raged. It roared.

He kissed her as if his life depended upon the union of their mouths. Somehow, they were moving. Dimly, he realized he was the one doing the moving, just as he had been the one to initiate the kissing. Because Miss Winter was moving backward and he was striding forward. His body was leaps ahead of his mind. Taking control. There was a bare expanse of wall where no pictures hung. And that was where he wanted her.

In four more strides, her back was pressed against the scarlet wallcovering. He broke the kiss and stared down at her, his chest heaving. He felt as if he had just run across a field. As if he had clambered to the top of a mountain, only to look out at the majesty of his height and wonder how the hell he would ever get back down.

Her lips were dark and swollen, parted. Her eyes were wide, glazed. She was clutching his biceps as if he were keeping her from slipping off a cliff. But if she thought he could save her from anything, including himself, she was bloody well wrong.

After eight-and-twenty years, he had finally kissed a woman.

And now that he had done so, he could not conceive of ever wanting to kiss another.

"I was right," said the maddening woman.

He was still not sure he could speak. But as usual, she had no difficulty holding up both ends of the exchange.

"About the use of tongues," she elaborated, her voice breathless. "I quite enjoyed your tongue in my mouth."

He groaned against a new bolt of lust, making his cock twitch. "I told you to stop saying that word, Miss Winter."

"Perhaps you ought to call me Christabella, Your Grace."

Yes, he could hardly continue to think of her in such proper terms when he wanted to make love to her against this wall, could he? *Damnation*, he was a scoundrel. He had always thought his brother was the rogue. But it seemed his inner rogue had just been released.

"Christabella," he said, forcing himself to remember he was a gentleman.

It was not an easy feat. All his honor had vanished the moment his lips had met hers.

"Much better." She smiled, revealing the dimple he found so alluring.

"If you do not leave this chamber in the next minute, I cannot promise I will not kiss you again," he warned.

"If you do not kiss me again, this will hardly be practice, will it?" she asked impishly.

As usual, she was no help.

And he wanted her all the more for it.

"If I do kiss you again, I am not certain I will be able to control myself," he felt compelled to warn.

"Now I am intrigued, Your Grace." Her grin deepened. "You must kiss me once more to satiate my curiosity."

"Gill," he told the minx, for he longed to hear his given name on her lips. But not as much as he longed to kiss her again.

Before she could respond, his mouth was on hers once more. He tried to be tender. To slow himself. But he was ravenous for her. All the years he had waited were worth it, for the revelation of her lips responding to his. For the miracle of her, teasing and tempting. She reached him in a way no other lady before her had.

He should be terrified, he thought. But instead, he felt free. He felt, in fact, unlike himself. So unlike himself, he caught her skirts in his hands, balling the soft fabric in his fists. He lifted it to her waist. Raised her hem as he fed from her lips. With one hand, he kept her gown trapped between them, raised to reveal her limbs. With his other, he explored. Sleek stockings, more feminine heat, her lush curves molding to his palm.

He sank his tongue deep into her mouth, gratified when she moaned and her fingers tunneled into his hair. He had no inkling if he was doing this properly. He was acting on instinct, listening to the sounds she made, paying attention to the subtle cues she gave. When she kissed him harder, he knew he was on the right path.

Just as he knew, when he dragged his palm past her garters, to the place where her stockings ended and her delicious bare skin began, that he was onto something very good indeed. Something wicked.

Something right.

He had seen a woman naked before. The courtesan Ash had paid to spend the night with him had worn nothing but a thin dressing gown, which she had removed. But he had not felt the tremendous burst of need he felt for Miss Winter—for Christabella. Instead, he had been terrified. His affliction had rendered him so ill at ease, he had been forced to withdraw from the chamber.

The lady had been paid well for her time and her silence.

It had been the sort of coin he and Ash could ill afford. And that had been the end of his brother's attempts to see him lose his cursed virginity. Gill was heartily glad for it now, because the uncomfortable interview paled in comparison to the sensation of Christabella in his arms, her lips moving against his, kissing him back with a fervor to match his own rampaging need. To the warmth of her inner thighs.

Good God.

The breath left him as he moved higher and she parted her legs to accommodate him. One moment, he was kissing her, stroking her leg. The next, he was about to spend in his breeches as his fingers met her most intimate flesh. Her mound was hot, covered in the silkiest thatch of hair. He cupped her there, knowing he should not. Knowing there was no way he could not.

Also, not knowing what the devil to do next.

She moved her head to the side, breaking the kiss, her breathing heavy and ragged. "Gill?"

His name.

Oh, Christ. She had said his name. And he was touching her cunny. Or something very near it. There was more to it than this, hidden facets he needed to explore. That much, he knew from the books he had read.

His cock was harder than coal.

He swallowed, then moved his fingers tentatively. He found a slit. Slick flesh. The discovery filled him with more roaring need. She moved her hips against him, bucking, seeking more, it seemed.

He rubbed his cheek against hers, inhaling the cloud of sweetness surrounding her coppery tresses. "Do you like that?"

"Yes."

Her sweet susurrus only served to inflame him more.

He parted her folds, his fingers seeking her pearl. When the pad of his forefinger brushed over the nub, she moaned her approval. He moved slowly at first, then with greater assurance. She seemed to prefer a faster pace, a less ginger touch.

Their cheeks were still pressed together, their bodies flush. There was just enough room between them to allow him to explore her. He wanted, with everything he had, to slide a finger inside her channel. Better yet, his cock. But he would not do it. Because he was not marrying Christabella Winter. She did not belong to him.

Why not, asked that blasted voice inside his head.

It was a fair question.

He needed funds. Christabella was a Winter. She was the only woman who had ever set him at ease. And he wanted her more than his next breath.

And so, it was without finesse or thought, and utterly without consideration, preparation, or the chance to weigh the merits of such a question at such a moment, and sadly without actually making Christabella spend, that he jerked his head back, and stared into her upturned face.

"Will you be my wife?" he found himself asking.

Almost as if another were speaking on his behalf.

He heard his voice as if he were detached from it. And he saw the surprise flare in Christabella's gaze, the passion give way to confusion.

"I beg your pardon?" she asked.

Good God, what a fool he was. He had touched his first cunny and had promptly asked the owner of said cunny to wed him. Worse, the lady in question looked neither impressed nor pleased.

His passion and his courage fled him.

He took a step in retreat, disengaging from her, releasing her skirts. Her hem fluttered to the floor, obscuring her stocking-clad legs from view. His fingers were still wet with her dew as he offered her a bow.

"Forgive me," he mumbled.

At least, he thought he did. The roaring in his ears was too much to withstand.

He turned and quit the chamber with all haste.

Chapter Five

CHRISTABELLA BLINKED AS the door to the red salon slammed closed, stealing from her the tempting sight of a broad, muscular back and long, lean legs striding away. Her mind, fogged as it was by desire, struggled to make sense out of what had occurred.

The Duke of Coventry had just kissed the breath out of her.

And then he had lifted her gown and touched her in precisely the place where she had stroked herself last night to thoughts of him.

It had been absolute bliss.

Until he had asked her to marry him.

With shaking hands, she smoothed the wrinkles from her skirts. A glance down at them revealed they were hopelessly crushed, the signs of what she had just been doing despicably evident. She would have to sneak back to her chamber for a change of gown without anyone being the wiser.

She should flee with what remained of her reputation still intact.

And yet, she could not seem to force herself to go.

Instead, her feet were moving, leading her across the chamber, and out the door. Chasing him, it seemed. Foolish as that was. Yes, she was running after Coventry—Gill—because he had looked distressed in the moment before he had retreated. And her reaction to his proposal had been, *well*, rude.

Because she had been shocked, of course, but he was not privy to her thoughts and could not know that. If his feelings were bruised by her words, she would never forgive herself. For she liked him, she was startled to realize as she continued her chase.

Very much.

But his legs were long, and his stride determined, she supposed. There was no sight of him up ahead in the west wing corridor. She rounded a bend and slammed straight into someone else.

Her sister, Pru.

They grasped each other's arms to keep from falling.

"Christabella, what has happened?" her eldest sister asked.

Oh, dear. If there was any of her sisters Christabella would have preferred to run across during her flight after she had nearly been ruined by a duke, Pru was not the one. She was sure she looked as if she had just been properly ravished. Because she had been. Delightfully so.

Not thoroughly enough.

Her cheeks went hot at the last thought.

"Nothing has happened," she lied at last, blinking. "Pru? What are you doing in this wing? I thought it rather uninhabited."

It was the reason she had chosen the red salon for her assignation with Coventry, after all.

"Have you just come from an assignation, Miss Christabella Mary Winter?" Pru demanded, invoking her dreaded second name.

Christabella felt her cheeks going hotter still. "No," she denied quickly.

Too quickly, she knew. Her sister was no fool. She could

see through any excuse. Cut right to the heart of a matter. And she was always playing mother hen, taking it upon herself to be the mother they were all lacking.

"You were meeting with someone," Pru pressed. "Tell me the truth."

The worst part about lying to her sister was that she was an abysmal liar. Also, she had no doubt she could not hold Pru's gaze whilst she fibbed. But there was no hope for it. Her mind and body yet reeled after what had just transpired in the red salon with Gill. She needed time to think about what she would do next.

She forced her gaze to a point over her sister's shoulder. "Of course I was not. I was merely seeking out some solitude. You are the one who practically knocked me off my feet. Where were *you* fleeing to in such haste?"

Indeed, now that she thought upon it, running into Pru in this wing of the house, also hurrying, was odd. She jerked her gaze back to her sister, noting she was flushed, and that tendrils of hair had escaped her coiffure.

"What happened to your hair?" Pru demanded, almost as if she had read Christabella's mind about herself. "It looks as if a man has been running his fingers through it."

Her hands flew to her hair, tentatively inspecting the damage Gill had wrought. "Perhaps I lost a hair pin. I was outside in the garden earlier, and it is quite windy."

A modicum of fibbing had never hurt anyone, after all.

"The wind did not steal a hair pin," her sister countered grimly, "and from the looks of it, you are missing more than one pin. I would wager at least five are gone, if not more."

Drat.

She patted her hair. "Perhaps it is from my bonnet, then. It did get caught in my hair when I was removing it."

"Why do you not tell me the truth?" Her sister's eyes

narrowed. "I am not a fool. I have eyes in my head. Your gown is wrinkled. Why, your skirts look as if they have been crushed."

Good God. Christabella thought of the manner in which her skirts had been crushed. And just how pleasant that interlude had been. She had known she ought to flee to her chamber to change her gown. And instead, she had gone running after Coventry, only to be caught.

"I fell in the gardens," she invented.

"Why is your gown not dirty?" Pru asked.

To the devil with persistent sisters who did not believe the lies they were fed.

She thought for a moment of a reason why, and settled upon one quickly.

"Because there is snow in the gardens." Christabella smiled, pleased with herself.

There. That ought to stifle her sister's questions. An unusually early winter's storm had blanketed the land in a dense coating of white. As unlikely as a fall into snow was, particularly since she was currently deep within the heart of Abingdon House, she had seized upon the idea.

"You expect me to believe your hair was ruined by the wind." Pru gave her a disapproving glare. "That the wind not only pulled your hat from your hair, but that it also plucked a handful of pins from it. And that after you were so mauled by the wind, leaving your hair half-unraveled down your back, you proceeded to fall into the snow in such a manner that your gown became hopelessly wrinkled. Much in the same fashion it would become wrinkled if it were raised to your waist?"

Drat and drat again.

Christabella returned the glare, reminding herself that Pru was in a similar state and that Gill's brother, the handsome, rakish Lord Ashley, had taken a marked interest in her. Could it be that the two sisters had been engaging in secret assignations with the brothers, each without the other being aware of it? At the least, she had to attempt to distract her sister with the idea.

"And how would you know what such wrinkles would look like, Pru? I confess, I cannot determine the difference between wrinkles caused by a Biblical fall and wrinkles caused by a literal fall. But if you can do so, pray, enlighten me."

Pru paled then.

"Did Lord Ashley Rawdon ravish you?" she asked.

Lord Ashley? Christbella frowned. She had supposed that was who Pru had been meeting, the reason for her mussed hair and dark lips. "Why should Lord Ashley want to ravish me?"

"If it was not Lord Ashley, then who was it?"

"No one ravished me," Christabella denied, deciding to stay with her original lie. "Truly, Pru. Did you not hear a word I just said? I was in the gardens—"

"Tell me the truth, Christabella, and tell me now," Pru interrupted.

Blast. She could not very well stand here all day, arguing with her sister, when anyone could come upon them. They both looked as if they had been properly ruined.

Christabella heaved a sigh. "Very well. I shall tell you, but you must promise not to go to our brother with this."

"I promise," Pru said. "Now out with it."

"It was the Duke of Coventry," Christabella admitted. "But he did not ravish me. Not at all. I was helping him."

Yes, that was how she preferred to think of it. Though in truth, somehow in the course of everything that had passed between them, she had forgotten she had been meant to aid him. She had forgotten everything but him, his kiss, his touch.

Lord God, his touch.

But now was decidedly not the time to recall the sensation of Gill's long fingers parting her flesh. Sending all those sparks shooting from the center of her being...

Pru's brows rose, her shock evident. "Coventry?"

Gill, she wanted to correct.

Wisely, she did not.

"Yes," she admitted.

Pru shook her head. "The Duke of Coventry? The man who scarcely speaks? *He* is the one who ravished you?"

"Hush!" Christabella cast a glance over her shoulder, hoping Gill was not lingering within earshot, or worse, eavesdropping. "Not so loud, if you please. Yes, it was he. But he did not ravish me, Pru. I swear it."

"You had better tell me everything, Christabella Mary Winter," Pru ordered. "Start at the beginning."

"There is nothing to tell." She linked her arm through her sister's, seeking a means of distraction. "I was just about to return to my chamber for a restorative nap."

"I will accompany you, but only in the name of keeping you from further trouble," said Pru. "On our way to the east wing, you can enlighten me as to how you have been *helping* him."

Oh, Christabella had no intention of telling her sister everything.

Just enough to satisfy her.

Certainly not that Gill had kissed her more passionately than she had ever dreamed a rake could. Nor that he had lifted her skirts to her waist. Definitely not the shocking pleasure of his touch on her most intimate flesh.

No, she would keep all that to herself.

"Charades," she said brightly as they walked along, seizing upon the first excuse that came to mind. "His Grace is terribly inept at playing the game, and it renders him quite nervous, you see. I offered to assist him in a practice game, of sorts."

Her explanation was not all that far from the truth.

"Charades," repeated Pru, her tone steeped in suspicion.

Well, mayhap it was.

"I am quite good at the game, as everyone knows," she continued with her fib. "Of course, His Grace enlisted my aid…"

THE FOLLOWING DAY, the sun did not shine any brighter upon his folly. But Gill was outdoors despite the cold, walking the holly maze with his brother. Largely because the out-of-doors seemed a place where he was unlikely to run across Miss Christabella Winter and embarrass himself by either kissing her or proposing to her again.

What a dolt he was.

He almost groaned aloud as he thought once more of his unpracticed attempts at seduction, followed by his inept offer of marriage.

She had refused him.

Of course she had, and she was doing the both of them a favor. Was she not?

Not, said a voice inside him. Devil take the voice.

Either way, now, he was not certain he could face her again.

He forced his mind back to the conversation he had been having with Ash.

"Miss Prudence wants to assist you with courting?" he asked.

This was an excellent sign, surely. At least he had the distraction of his brother, who had fallen neatly into the trap Gill had laid for him. Ash was a rakehell of the first order, but since their arrival at the country house party, Ash had been watching Miss Prudence Winter, the eldest of the Winter sisters. Gill had decided to put his suspicions to the test.

And seeing as how he had stumbled upon Ash and Miss Prudence alone in the wake of his disastrous assignation with Christabella, he was beginning to believe he had been correct. His scoundrel brother was falling in love.

Just as well that one of them was.

That one of them could find happiness.

Lord knew happiness was not for Gill. It was one of the reasons he wanted to see his brother married. Because if Ash was wed and settled down, Gill would not have to fret over his own marriage. He would simply marry an heiress—any heiress—and live a comfortable, separate life from her.

At least, that was what he had thought.

Until Miss Christabella Winter had entered his life.

"She offered me aid in observing the proprieties when courting ladies," Ash said slowly then, his tone hesitant, almost as if he hated to reveal the information. "Yes."

Gill laughed at the notion of Ash and respectability, which had never before belonged in the same sentence. Yes indeed, these were all good signs. Miss Prudence had found a rake in need of reforming, and she had settled upon Ash. "Does she not know you do not give a damn about propriety?"

"Perhaps she thinks she is performing a service for her fellow sex," Ash returned lightly. "It matters not, for I only agreed so that I might get a bit more acquainted with her and determine whether or not the two of you would suit."

"Selfless of you, brother," Gill teased, relieved to turn his mind to lighter matters and away from the embarrassment threatening to swallow him whole.

"I have not compromised her, if that is what you are

implying," snapped Ash.

Ah, brother. Methinks thou doth protest too much.

"I did come upon the two of you in the salon," he pointed out. "Alone. Miss Winter seemed rather flushed."

And after what he had been about in a nearby salon, Gill knew all about a flushed Winter lady. A very different flushed Winter lady.

The one he had thought about all night long. And all morning. And almost every minute since…

Something landed in the center of his chest quite suddenly. He looked down to discover the remnants of a snowball upon his greatcoat.

What the devil?

"Oh dear," said a feminine voice he would recognize anywhere. "Do forgive me, Your Grace. I fear my aim was misplaced."

Christabella.

He should have known.

He glanced up to find her blue-green eyes dancing with mischief. How had he expected anything less? Was she laughing at him? With him? Did she always react to a proposal of marriage by pelting the gentleman with snowballs?

"Forgive my sister, Your Grace," Miss Prudence Winter called. "She did not intend to hit you with the snowball. Are you injured?"

He was not certain if it was the cold rendering him speechless at the moment, his affliction, or shock. Either way, he could not seem to speak.

"Actually, I did mean to hit you," Christabella said then, grinning her minx's grin and revealing that damned dimple. "But I was aiming for your hat."

He found his tongue at last. "That was a childish prank, madam."

Her grin did not diminish. Her cheeks were rosy from the cold. There was no doubt she was enjoying this, the maddening woman.

"Forgive me, Your Grace," she said without a hint of contrition in her voice. "As you know, I am beset by an inability to behave."

He choked out a laugh. Truer words had never been spoken. And yet, as had become common, her impish nature lightened the weight which had settled upon his chest. He may have bungled his attempt at asking her to be his duchess the day before. However, as he stood there in the sunlit garden, surrounded by frigid December air, their siblings looking on, the remnants of her snowball stuck to his coat, he made a decision.

He was going to marry this minx.

But first, he was going to retaliate in kind.

He sank to his haunches, formed a snowball, and then took careful aim. The snowball hit her bonnet and broke, sending snow raining down into her face.

"Oh, you bounder!" Christabella exclaimed. "That was one of my best hats!"

He found himself grinning back at her. "I was merely showing you an example of excellent aim, Miss Winter."

"That is the outside of enough. I declare this a war. Pru, start making snowballs," she ordered her sister.

Miss Prudence began to protest when Ash threw a snowball, entering the melee. The missile hit her bonnet, interrupting her chastisement.

"Did you dare to throw a snowball at me, Lord Ashley?" she demanded.

"Yes, I did," Ash called back. "Your sister announced this is war, after all. We must defend ourselves."

A full snow battle ensued. Before long, the four of them

were laughing, flinging snowballs at each other, and generally acting more like a quartet of children than the adults they were. As snow was flung at them from every direction, Gill met his brother's gaze.

"I say we go in separate directions and try to lose them," he said as another snowball landed on his chest.

"Excellent idea," Ash agreed, dodging another burst of snow.

They turned and raced through the slippery snow, heading deeper into the maze. When they reached a wall of holly, Gill and Ash parted, with Gill heading to the left and Ash to the right. He could only hope the sisters followed and that, even better, the right sister chose his path.

He stopped when he reached a statue of Venus, the air cold in his lungs.

In the next instant, Christabella came careening toward him, her bonnet askew, cheeks even more flushed, her infectious giggle hitting him in the chest with the same force as her snowball. She slid in the snow just before she reached him, and he caught her in his arms, holding her there.

My God, she was lovely.

She took his breath.

He stared down into her dancing eyes, remembering his ill-timed proposal and the cowardly fashion in which he had run from her the day before. He ought to say something, he knew. If only he knew what.

She spared him by touching his cheek. Her gloved fingers were coated in snow, sending the strangest combination of heat and cold through him all at once. "I like your smile," she said softly, disarming him utterly.

She made him smile. Her mischievousness nature was infectious.

"I cannot recall the last time I ever threw a snowball," he

said.

And wished he had not. He should have taken the opportunity to woo her. To somehow make amends for his foolish offer yesterday.

"You are too serious, Gill." Her fingertips traced over his mouth.

Snow melted on his bottom lip. He wished she were not wearing gloves. He wanted her skin on his.

He settled for pressing a kiss to her fingertips, impeded by the barrier between them. "I am sorry."

Her gaze searched his. "You should not be sorry for being too serious. You should smile more. Throw more snowballs."

An easy solution.

He swallowed past a sudden lump in his throat. What would his life be like, with this unpredictable woman as his duchess?

One word, he thought.

Wonderful.

But how to persuade her? He would have to do better than he had yesterday, ravishing her against a wall and muttering a proposal.

"Perhaps I should practice kissing more," he said, his voice low. "I find the act far more pleasing than throwing snow."

Her lips parted. "Oh, yes. I do think you might also practice a bit more."

He took that as an invitation.

And then he took her lips. The kiss was tentative at first. A mere joining. He was tense, the stakes were higher, the day was bright. They were out-of-doors, though hidden by the sculpted evergreen of the holly bushes. Still, Ash and Miss Prudence were just around the bend. And perhaps others were about.

Kissing her was dangerous.

But he was desperate for her mouth.

The need for her won over all else. Caution was forgotten when she kissed him back, her arms twining around his neck. Her tongue touched his. He groaned, licking into her mouth as the kiss quickly turned carnal.

He ended it before he lost control of himself. He could not press her into the prickly bushes the same way he had pinned her to the wall yesterday. Moreover, he had no desire for his brother to happen upon him whilst he was in the midst of ruining a lady. Nor did he have a wish to ruin Christabella.

He wanted to marry her.

They stared at each other for a heavy moment, silence broken only by the sound of voices in the distance. It was all the reminder he needed. Carefully, he set her away from him.

"We should rejoin my brother and your sister," he said.

"Must we?" Her grin was teasing.

He wanted to kiss her again, but he did not dare trust himself. Instead, he sank to his haunches and scooped up another ball of snow.

"I surrender," she said, giggling again.

She was too late. He had already tossed the snowball softly, his aim perfect.

It broke open directly over her heart.

Chapter Six

THE DUKE OF Coventry had thrown a snowball at her heart.

Surely it held significance?

Surely not.

Or did it?

With each step, she changed her mind.

It meant something.

It did not.

It meant something.

It did not.

Of course it did. He had proposed to her two days ago in the west wing. Not that she wanted to marry him. For of course she did not. She was meant to marry a wicked rake, not a man who had never before kissed a lady. Then again, for a novice at kissing, he had certainly learned enough to rob her breath…

Christabella sighed as she tramped to the breakfast room the next morning. She was so lost in her thoughts that she did not see the lady rushing down the hall from the opposite direction until it was too late. They collided, the impact sending them both to their rumps. Christabella attempted to catch herself and twisted her ankle quite viciously on her way down.

"Oh," was all Christabella could think to say, rubbing her

smarting bottom as her gaze settled upon the lady she had crashed into. "I am so sorry, my lady."

Lady Adele Saltisford was a shy, quiet wallflower.

The daughter of a duke.

Rather the sort of woman Christabella imagined would suit Gill. Aristocratic, pretty, and with an ice to rival his own. The thought had her grimacing as she rose to her feet and offered Lady Adele a hand. Not just grimacing. It sent an unwanted pang to her heart. Something akin to pain.

But then another pain entirely shot straight through her. Beginning with her ankle and shooting, white-hot, up her leg.

"Forgive me, Miss Winter," Lady Adele said, looking flustered. "The fault is all mine, I am afraid. I was not watching where I was going."

"I was not watching either, my lady." Christabella felt guilty for her lack of circumspection, even as the pain throbbed. She had been every bit as responsible for what had happened as Lady Adele.

She had been gadding about like a whirlwind, thinking only of herself, after all.

And Gill.

Of course, Gill.

Er, the Duke of Coventry.

Lady Adele gained her feet as well and brushed at her skirts, wincing. "Are you in pain, my dear? Have I injured you with my thoughtlessness?"

"I am perfectly fine, Lady Adele," she lied, gritting her teeth. "Please, do not allow me to keep you from your destination."

Lady Adele frowned at her. "But you look rather pale. And I do believe I saw you limping, just now."

"Nonsense." Christabella forced a smile. "I was not limping at all. You have nothing to fret over, my lady. I shall be fine."

Lady Adele had been traveling somewhere in haste, that much was certain. She had a twin sister, and an older, widowed sister accompanying her at the house party. But neither of those two ladies were in sight. Christabella was curious what was making Lady Adele run. But the insistent pain in her ankle reminded her she had far greater worries of her own to attend to.

"You are certain?" Lady Adele asked.

Christabella noted she seemed rather pale. Perhaps she was ill? Either way, Christabella had no wish for Lady Adele to feel responsible for her twisted ankle, especially since she was as much to blame.

"Certain." Her smile felt more strained than ever. Almost as painful as the aching in her limb. "Thank you for your concern."

Absolved of her culpability, and still looking as if she were about to cast up her accounts, Lady Adele apologized once more, before continuing down the hall as if the hounds of hell were nipping at her heels. Alone once more, Christabella took a deep breath and strode forward.

The pain in her ankle radiated through her, making her gasp.

Oh, dear.

This was not good.

Not good at all.

A glance over her shoulder confirmed Lady Adele had disappeared from sight. There was no one about to offer her aid. Feeling ill herself, she leaned against the wall, alongside a portrait of one of her sister-in-law, Lady Emilia's, ancestors. A dour-faced man sporting a ruff and an expression of disapproval. He looked as if he had scented dung, she thought rather unkindly.

Someone ought to have thrown a snowball or two at him. Perhaps he would have smiled for his portrait.

But she needed to attempt another few steps, at least. To find her way to the breakfast table. Her stomach rumbled in agreement at the thought.

Pushing herself away from the wall, she took another step. Then another.

The pain was outrageous. She started hopping on her good foot.

And of course that was when the Duke of Coventry rounded the bend, finding her limping about like a wounded hare.

He stopped where he stood, offering her a formal bow that belied the last time their paths had crossed, during their impromptu snowball fight. He had been laughing, lighthearted. She had chased after him, delighting in the sight of him so free, so joyous.

She felt none of that delight now. Only irritation.

"What are you doing here, Your Grace?" she asked.

Was it not bad enough that he dominated all her thoughts? That he had threatened everything she thought she knew about herself? Now he must also appear when she was wounded?

"Walking to the stables after breaking my fast, of course," he told her, startling her with his instant response. "Why are you hopping on one foot?"

He had witnessed her ignominy in full, it would seem.

Oh, how wonderful.

Would it have been too much to ask that he pretended she was walking in an ordinary fashion?

"I seem to have twisted my ankle," she admitted reluctantly. "It is rather tender at the moment, so I was seeking to keep the weight from it."

"Good God, woman, why did you not say so immediately?" He strode forward, closing the distance between them.

Before she could protest, he had lifted her effortlessly into his strong arms.

And once she was there, she could not recall how to form a single protest anyway. Her arms wound around his neck. Being in his arms was...

She searched her mind for a suitable description.

Shocking. Improper.

Wicked. Delicious.

"You cannot carry me to breakfast in such fashion," she chastised all the same. "It will be quite the scandal."

"I can do what I wish," he argued mulishly.

"You can," she allowed, trying to ignore the masculine scent of him, along with the urge to kiss his stubborn mouth. "But you should not. Indeed, you must not."

Now that she had known the pleasure of his kiss, she could not seem to stop wanting more. But the Duke of Coventry was altogether wrong for her. Just as she was altogether wrong for him. She wanted a rake. A man who knew how to seduce and thrill and show her the heights of passion.

He frowned at her now. "If you do not want me to carry you there, then where shall I take you, my dear?"

My dear.

Those two words should not send heat flooding to her core. And yet, in his deep voice, his strong arms tight around her as if he would hold her forever there, they did.

This was getting dangerous. The longer they lingered here in the hall where anyone could come across them, the greater their chance of creating a scandal.

"There is a writing room, just over there," she said, nodding toward the closed door with her head. Not because she did not wish to release her hold on his neck, of course.

But his hair was so soft. Soft and thick. He was like a tall, golden warrior. A beautiful, patrician duke with the body of a man who labored for his bread. And clinging to him felt nothing short of wondrous.

Very well, she did not wish to release her hold on his neck.

Because clinging to him made her feel secure and aflame all at once.

"Third door on the left?" he asked, moving in the direction of her nod.

"Yes," she answered simply. For what else was there to say?

He was silent as he stalked to the door in question, and she took the opportunity to observe him. His jaw was rigid, his stare straight ahead. What a strange sensation, being carried in a man's arms. She felt as if she were floating. And in this man's arms, in particular...

They made it through the door, which he managed with one-handed aplomb, and then he carried her to a divan. The writing room was blessedly empty, the door closed at their backs. As he lowered her to the cushion, she knew a keen surge of disappointment.

Regret.

She hated to let go of him.

But she must, and so she did, but still, the duke did not move. He was near, hovering over her. Close enough to kiss. She told herself she would not move. Would not press her mouth to his, no matter how tempting such a notion may be. She told herself she would not give in.

"Thank you," she said, hating how breathless she sounded. Hating how much he affected her. He was not supposed to make her want him so, this icy man who was the opposite of a rake.

And yet, he did.

She found his silence endearing.

She found his kisses entrancing.

And the way he had touched her the other day, beneath her gown…

"May I see your ankle?" he rasped.

Those eyes, brighter than a country summer's cloudless sky, burned into hers. Their faces remained indecently near. It was as if neither one of them wanted to end this moment, the sorcery of their aloneness.

She forgot his question. She was confused. And famished, but not just for eggs and hothouse pineapple any longer. Rather, for this man. For the Duke of Coventry.

Gill.

He quirked a golden brow. "Yes?"

What a daft chit she was. Had she said his name aloud?

"You ought to go," she told him, even if it was the last thing she wished. "Tell my sister Pru where I am, and she can aid me."

His gaze searched hers. "I cannot leave you if you are in pain."

Could he kiss her? She could not help but wonder.

Although she knew quite well she should not.

This is not the man for you, she reminded herself. Even if he did propose. And even if he had thrown a snowball at her heart, as if he were declaring war upon that particular part of her. Even if she could think of nothing but his mouth on hers, his long fingers seeking her flesh…

This was not going well.

He seemed to be looking at her expectantly. Was it her turn to speak? What had he said last? Her ankle was aching, it was true, but it was nothing compared to the other ache. The other need.

"Why are you still here?" she asked.

They had pushed the boundaries of propriety—heavens, if she were honest, they had trampled over them like runaway horses—before. But that had been in a chamber where it had been far less likely they would ever be intruded upon. Not within a heavily used room, just out of earshot of the dining room where their fellow guests broke their fasts.

She did not want to be forced into marriage. Or ruined, she reminded herself. No matter how deliciously wicked the Duke of Coventry made her feel.

"You are injured," he said, his tone concerned, his brow furrowed. "I cannot leave you in such a state."

The state she was in had far more to do with the man before her than with her ankle, and that was the truth. What would the harm be, the wickedest part of her wondered, in keeping him here with her? In basking in his presence, his touch, just for a few moments more?

She could not.

She dared not.

Did she?

She thought of the snowball hitting her heart, the expression upon his handsome face.

Oh, yes, she dared.

"There is a way you could help my ankle to feel better," she said before her rational mind attempted to divert her from her course.

"Tell me," he urged.

"Kiss me," she said.

"Kiss me," Christabella told him.

Gill stared into her face. Into her beautiful, haunting, lovely face. Into her blue-green eyes. He tried to remind himself his original purpose in bringing her here, to this chamber, alone. Tried to recall she was injured, that she had somehow hurt her ankle and had been in true pain when he had first come upon her in the hall.

But all he could think about was her lips.

About taking them again.

"You are hurt," the gentleman within him protested. "Allow me to tend you. To make certain you have not done yourself serious injury."

Still, he did not make an effort to put more distance between them. One dip of his head, and he could claim her mouth as his own. Which it was, because he was going to make her his duchess. He was decided upon his path.

"I think we need to continue our lessons," she said, her voice low. Husky.

Sensual.

His cock, already hard, twitched.

"Lessons?" Mindlessly, he drew nearer, as if he were a bee drawn to the blossom.

There was almost no distance between them. He was on his knees before her, his body pressed to her limbs. He wondered if she could feel the effect she had upon him, even through the layers of his breeches and her petticoats and gown.

Eight-and-twenty years he had remained a virgin, and yet he had never felt so tempted, so desperate, as he did now. As if he would explode if he did not have her. Or at least touch her. If he did not raise her skirts and place his mouth upon her where he truly wished. Upon that slick flesh he had scarcely been able to pleasure two days ago. Upon her cunny.

"Our kissing lessons," Christabella elaborated then, her

hands fluttering back to his shoulders.

Her touch was hesitant. Encouraging.

He inhaled swiftly against a bolt of pure, unadulterated lust. His ballocks were drawn tight. The cloud of her scent enveloped him, summery and bright. She smelled like the garden of temptation. And how ironic that was, for she was his temptress, his call to sin.

He would not regret a single damned moment of sinning with this woman, and he knew it.

"Kissing lessons," he repeated, because his mind had largely ceased to function. But pretending to misunderstand her did nothing to abate the problem.

There was only one solution: lips and tongue and teeth.

"Yes," she agreed, stroking his shoulders. "Those."

He forgot her ankle was injured for a moment. Forgot everything but her acquiescence and her lips. Her plump, ripe lips, so pink, so delicious, so ready for the taking. And take he did. He slammed his mouth against hers. No finesse. He was still learning. Also, he was ravenous.

Christabella did not seem to mind.

She moaned into his mouth, opening beneath his neophyte onslaught. Their tongues met. Her fingers sank into his hair. They kissed and kissed and kissed. Until he moved her, and she emitted a small sound of dismay.

It was enough.

He pulled away, reminded of her twisted ankle.

"Forgive me," he said, trying to gather his thoughts. "It was not my intention to—"

"Hush." She pressed her forefinger against his lips, canceling further words. "Do not apologize for kissing me. Never apologize for that."

He kissed the fleshy pad.

She ran her fingertip over his upper lip first, then the

lower, her expression one of mesmerized fascination. Fire swept through him, starting where she touched him and licking down his spine, spreading everywhere.

"Your mouth is lovely," she said.

No one had ever told him such a thing before. He wanted to speak, but all that emerged was a strangled sound. It was not his affliction, he thought. But rather the maddening effect this woman had upon him. He would happily remain on his knees, allowing her to touch his lips, for the rest of his days.

"Why do you have to be so handsome?" she asked him then, frowning as if he had displeased her.

He thought he had an agreeable face and form, but he was no rakehell like his brother. Ladies did not chase after him. He swallowed. Tried to think of something else to say.

Ah, yes.

The ankle.

"Shall I tend to your ankle now?" he asked.

"It is nothing," she said. "I twisted it when I collided with Lady Adele."

Despite her protestations, he knew it must have pained her. What a beast he was, kissing her when she had an injury. What had he been thinking?

Grimly, he took her hand in his and placed it in her lap. "Let me have a look."

Before she could protest, he lifted the hem of her gown and petticoats, careful not to raise it too high lest he tempt himself any further. Her ankles were a thing of wonder, covered in white stockings, dainty and feminine. *Good God*, who had thought a woman's feet could be alluring? Certainly not Gill, but the sight of Christabella Winter's slippers and curved calves were setting his heart pounding.

He forced himself to recall which ankle she had been favoring, then gently took up her left foot. It did not appear to be swollen. He moved her foot slowly, first one way, then the other.

Gill glanced up at her. "How does that feel?"

"The pain is a bit higher," she told him.

He allowed his hands to glide up her calf. "Here?"

"Higher."

He reached her knee, desire burning anew. "Here?"

Her pink tongue darted over the lushness of her lower lip. "Higher."

Was she trying to kill him? He had just determined not to be improper. He ought to lower her skirts, step away from her. Leave the chamber. But he was ensnared, falling into her eyes, his fingers traveling higher of their own accord. To the place where her stockings ended.

There, he hesitated, grazing warm, silken, womanly flesh.

"Christabella," he said her name on a groan.

Because from here, there was not far to go until he reached her quim.

And that was all he could bloody well think about.

Until the door to the writing room swung open.

Chapter Seven

*T*HE SHOCKED GASP of Lady Adele cut through the silence of the writing room.

Christabella's heart was suddenly pounding for a reason that had nothing to do with Gill's hands upon her bare skin. Her gaze shot to Lady Adele's. The door was ajar behind her, but the hall appeared to be clear. Meaning there was only one witness to the Duke of Coventry's hands beneath her gown.

Unfortunately, the divan upon which he had settled her faced the entry, which meant Lady Adele had an unfettered view of Gill on his knees before her, hems raised to her knees.

"Forgive me," Lady Adele said, her countenance pale. "I did not mean to intrude."

Gill flipped her gown down, then stood, towering over Christabella and blocking her from view. He bowed, as if they had not just been caught engaged in shockingly inappropriate behavior.

"Lady Adele," he said.

And then said nothing else.

Oh, dear. He was not helping matters.

Christabella peered around his imposing form. "His Grace was helping me with my—"

"Torn hem," Gill blurted, shocking her by speaking.

"Yes," she lied, hoping Lady Adele could not see her flawlessly intact hem around Gill's imposing body. "And he was just about to fetch my sister for me. Were you not, Your Grace?"

"Yes," he said, his voice wooden. "Er, yes."

He bowed again, and then he stalked from the room, saying nothing more. Christabella winced as he retreated as if he were fleeing a burning building. In some ways, perhaps he was. Her gown was now on full display for Lady Adele's inspection. Christabella debated the merits of running herself, sore ankle or no, when the other woman glided across the chamber and settled onto the divan at her side.

"I am so sorry for bumping into you," Lady Adele said. "And you need not fear I will tell anyone what I saw just now."

What she had seen had been scandalous.

Christabella knew it.

Just as she knew it could prove her ruin. If Lady Adele were to speak a word to anyone, Christabella would find herself the next Duchess of Coventry.

Why did the prospect not fill her with dread? Why did it instead fill her with a strange feeling of rightness?

"It was not as wicked as it looked," she offered lamely.

Which was a lie, of course.

For it *had* been wicked. And wonderful, too.

"Your secret is safe with me," Lady Adele assured her, giving her hand a pat. "It is the least I can do after being so clumsy. I confess, I turned back to see if you were well, and I saw His Grace carrying you into this chamber. When some time had passed, and you had not emerged, I reasoned it best to make my presence known, before someone else happened upon you."

Had Lady Adele seen more than Gill with his hands beneath her gown?

Christabella felt ill. "It is not…we were not…"

"You need not explain, Miss Winter," Lady Adele interrupted. "Nor should you fret. I will reassure everyone that after we collided in the hall, His Grace immediately left to seek your sister whilst I stayed here by your side. The two of you were never alone."

She eyed Lady Adele. "You would lie for me."

"I would offer an explanation far more suitable than the truth," Lady Adele corrected, her tone gentle.

"Why, my lady?" she asked bluntly. "Doing so would offer you no benefit."

Lady Adele smiled, but there was no joy in it, only sadness. "Oh, but it would. For I have a favor to ask of you."

A favor? Now this was indeed intriguing. Christabella could not fathom what manner of favor she could perform for a lovely duke's daughter.

"Whatever can it be?" she asked.

But before she could answer, her elder sister, Pru, swept into the chamber. "Christabella Mary Winter, what manner of trouble have you managed to find yourself in now?" she demanded.

Christabella sighed at the disapproval in her sister's voice. And then she did the only thing she could do—she lied. "No trouble at all."

GILL NEEDED TO exercise caution.

He knew it.

If he wanted to make Christabella Winter his wife, he had to stop taking such foolish risks with her reputation. Kissing her in every chamber of Abingdon House and raising her skirts as if he were a practiced seducer of innocents had to stop.

He chastised himself all the way to her chamber.

Then he cautioned himself some more whilst he stood there.

He knocked anyway, of course.

It had been hours since he had last left Christabella in the care of Lady Adele and fetched her sister, Miss Prudence Winter. During the course of the afternoon, Miss Prudence had been absent from the drawing room entertainments arranged by their hostess, Lady Emilia. As had Ash.

The significance of the two being gone simultaneously had not been lost upon Gill.

Nor had it aided him in his quest to see how Christabella was faring. Since she, too, had failed to appear this afternoon, and since Ash and Miss Prudence were nowhere to be found, he had no choice. That was his reasoning for seeking out her chamber in the midst of the day.

He was concerned for her wellbeing.

"You may enter," Christabella called.

He hesitated.

What if her lady's maid were within? Or someone else?

Devil take it, he had not thought this scenario out in its entirety, had he?

No, he had not. But it was too late to allow that to stop him now. He opened the door and stepped over the threshold.

The chamber was as elegantly appointed as his, decorated with pastoral paintings and pale-blue wall coverings. He found Christabella at once, seated in a settee by the hearth, her leg propped upon a footstool. She had been engrossed in a book, but she looked up at his entrance, her countenance startled.

"What are you doing here?" she asked, snapping her book closed, color staining her cheeks.

That was not precisely the welcome he had been hoping for, either.

"It is familiar of me, I realize," he said, feeling his chest constrict and his heart begin pounding.

Damnation, all he needed was for his affliction to hit him now.

"It is very familiar," she said, stuffing the book she had been reading beneath her rump.

Curious, that. The action was so odd, in fact, that it distracted him enough to rein in his madly galloping emotions.

"Are you sitting on your book?" he asked, genuinely perplexed.

The color in her cheeks heightened.

"No."

He cocked his head. "I saw you stow it beneath your bottom just now, Christabella."

She huffed a little sigh, looking somehow extra lovely in her pique. "What I have done with my book matters not when you are going about, invading my chamber in the midst of the day. What if someone were to see you?"

"No one saw me." At least, he did not think anyone saw him.

Wisely, he kept that thought to himself.

"We are fortunate indeed that Lady Adele has promised not to tell anyone what she witnessed earlier," Christabella said. "Now, here you are again, tempting fate."

He was tempting everything, and most especially himself, with his presence here. Still, he did not go.

"I came to inquire after your ankle," he told her, belatedly offering her a bow.

He was not certain of the proper etiquette for visiting an unwed lady in her chamber. But at the very least, genuflection was in order.

"It is well enough, thank you," she said, her voice uncharacteristically prim.

"Good." He nodded, knowing he should leave before anyone found him within her chamber.

Instead, he moved closer, drawn to her as ever.

"Gill," she protested. "What are you doing?"

"Sitting alongside you," he answered as he settled at her side.

The warm scent of summer blossoms greeted him.

Divine.

"You should not be here." Her voice was soft, almost hushed.

"I know." He felt stiff and out of place. Part of him wondered why he had sought her out at all. For it was foolish and reckless, as she had so rightly pointed out.

And he had never been foolish.

Nor reckless.

At least, he had not been until he had crossed paths with Miss Christabella Winter.

"However, I am glad you are here."

Her confession startled him, but not nearly as much as her next action did. She took his hand in hers and laced their fingers together, so that their palms touched. Rather like a kiss. And his heart seemed to clench in his chest.

The gesture was so easy.

So affectionate.

No woman had ever touched him thus. Somehow, it seemed more intimate than a kiss. He struggled to find words.

"You are?" was all he could manage.

"Yes." She gave his fingers a squeeze. "Even though you pelted me with snowballs yesterday."

His lips quirked into a grin. How did she always set him so at ease, make him smile?

"As I recall it, you fired the first shot," he told her, staring down at their interlaced fingers.

Her hand was easily dwarfed in his.

"You must admit you had fun," she teased, playfully bumping her shoulder against his.

He glanced down at her, into her upturned face, and he could think of nothing but kissing her. Making her his. Of her becoming his duchess. He was firm in his decision. This was the woman he wanted at his side.

In his bed.

"I will admit I had fun," he allowed, "in exchange for you telling me why you are sitting on your book."

She pursed her lips. "Perhaps it is because I wish to keep it warm."

He laughed. She was ridiculous, and he found her intoxicating.

Strangely, maddeningly, intoxicating.

"I did not realize paper and leather require warming," he said.

"Oh yes." She nodded, continuing her ruse. "I cannot bear to read a cold book. So difficult to turn the pages, you understand."

"What I understand is that I am having the silliest conversation I have ever had." He raised a brow at her. "You cannot be comfortable, sitting upon a hard book."

"I am wonderfully comfortable." Her lips twitched as if she were stifling laughter.

"What else do you sit upon?" he could not resist teasing. "Pray tell me you do not sit upon small dogs or teacups to keep them warm."

She did laugh then. Her laughter was tinkling and beautiful, and it sent a bolt of need straight through him. "Why those choices, of all things?"

"They were the first that came to mind." He was smiling with her, falling into her eyes all over again.

Her gaze searched his, and whatever she saw there made her levity fade. "I only sit upon books and seats, I promise."

He gave her fingers another squeeze. "Do you sit upon all your books, or just books you are seeking to hide from me?"

"Why should you think I am seeking to hide it from you?" she countered.

Easy answer for that one. "You are sitting on it."

She was staring at his mouth now. "You do know you are behaving in scandalously improper fashion by sitting with me here in my chamber, do you not?"

He wondered if she was thinking about the kisses they had shared, and tamped down a wave of longing. "I do. However, I deemed the risk worthwhile, considering I had no other means of knowing how you fared. Your absence left me concerned."

She raised a brow. "You could have asked my sister, Pru."

He cleared his throat. "She was not present at the afternoon's entertainments."

Christabella frowned. "That is odd. When she left here earlier, she said she was going directly to the drawing room."

All the more reason to suppose Miss Prudence had arranged for an assignation with his rakehell of a brother.

"She is a good woman, your sister?" he asked, feeling a surge of protectiveness for Ash, whom he knew so often felt the same way about him, thanks to his affliction. "Kindhearted?"

Christabella smiled fondly. "Oh, yes. She has the kindest of hearts. There is none better. Why do you ask?"

He shifted in his seat, growing uncomfortable. "No reason."

Her eyes narrowed. Christabella Winter was no fool. "Tell me."

Damnation. Now he would have to share his plan with

her. What if she told Miss Prudence and the whole affair was muddled?

He considered his options.

"Gill," she prodded sternly.

"I will tell you, as long as you promise me you shall carry it no further," he said at last. "You can tell no one. Not any of your sisters. Do you promise?"

"Not even my sisters?" She pursed her lips, rendering them all the more kissable. "But they are my best friends."

The Winter family was notorious in many ways, one of which was their fierce protectiveness over one another. Her objection came as no surprise. But he remained firm. He wanted happiness for Ash, and he was not about to allow anyone to ruin it. Even if she was the most delicious creature he had ever beheld.

"Not even them," he insisted.

She sighed. "Very well. I do hate secrets. I cannot bear to go on now, knowing you are keeping something from me. I promise I shall not tell my sisters. What is it?"

"I am playing matchmaker, of sorts," he revealed, feeling silly by the mere utterance of the words aloud.

For after all, he knew nothing of courting. Until this house party and Christabella, he had never kissed a lady. Who was he to believe he could play matchmaker for his brother? To win a lady for his brother, who was handsome and charming and who knew how to make a lady fall into his bed with the mere quirk of a well-timed eyebrow?

"Matchmaker," Christabella repeated slowly, blinking. "You?"

"Yes." His ears were hot. As were his cheeks. He wondered if he were flushing. Gill fidgeted with his cravat, suddenly feeling as if it were too restrictive. "My brother is a good man. He has spent far too much time fretting over me and my—my affliction. Indeed, his presence at this house party is down to his desire to aid me, for I am the one who is in search of a bride. But I saw the way he looked at your sister, Miss Prudence. And I made a wager with him that he could not woo the lady of my choosing on my behalf. I chose your sister. He believes he is courting her for me."

Her frown returned, this time quite fiercely. "Lord Ashley is courting Pru on your behalf?"

"He *thinks* he is," Gill repeated, hastening to reassure her. "In truth, my interest lies elsewhere. But Ash believes he is happy devoting his life to being a ne'er-do-well second son, luring London's ladies out of their gowns."

"Well he is most certainly not allowed to woo my sister out of her gown!" Christabella's outrage echoed in the chamber as she released his hand. "She is a respectable lady, even if she is a Winter."

Blast. It seemed he was muddling this up well enough on his own.

He took her hand back in his. "I am not encouraging him to ruin her, Christabella. I would never do such a thing. I want to see him married to her."

That rather took the vinegar out of her expression. "Oh. But Pru does not want to get married to anyone."

"Perhaps she will change her mind," he said pointedly. "Did you not see the way the two of them were looking at each other after our snowball fight in the gardens?"

She was silent for a beat, apparently mulling over her recollections. "Yes, I did. And now that you mention it, she did look awfully mussed and rumpled when I bumped into her in the hall the other day. As if she had been thoroughly kissed…"

"He will do the honorable thing by her," he vowed. For he knew his brother. Rakehell though he may be, Ash was a gentleman. And he did have honor. He had simply needed to find the right woman.

Just as Gill had. For altogether different reasons, of course.

"He had better," Christabella warned, "or I shall be forced to enact revenge upon him."

He was sure he did not want to know what Christabella Winter's idea of revenge was.

"He will," he reaffirmed.

She gave him a hard look. "Is my sister alone with him now?"

"I do not know." That, at least, was complete honesty. He knew not where the devil Ash had gone. All he did know was that neither Miss Prudence nor his brother had been present in the drawing room earlier.

"Gill." She squeezed his hand, as if in warning.

"Christabella." He squeezed back and thought about kissing her, to erase all the questions from her sweet lips.

How odd it was to think their mouths had met. That he had held her in his arms. That he spoke to her, without the affliction rendering him mute. So much had changed in the course of this house party.

Everything had changed.

She was watching him now, her stare curious. Probing. Intense.

He stared back, and his heart pounded, but not with anxiety. Rather, with sensual intent. Their palms remained sealed, fingers laced.

"If Lord Ashley is a rotten cad, I will never forgive you for your interference," she warned.

"He is not a rotten cad." On this, he was certain.

Just as he was certain that he was about to kiss her yet again.

"But I do think it is sweet of you to want to see your brother happily settled." She paused, eying him shrewdly. "And I do think it was sweet of you to check on me, even if you should never have come here to my chamber."

Progress, so it seemed.

"How is your ankle?" he asked again, for he had not forgotten her injury.

A small smile flirted with her lips. "It only pains me when I stand on it for too long. I am quite able to walk about, however. Fortunately, the damage was of a temporary rather than permanent nature."

"Pity," he said, eying her mouth. "I rather enjoyed carrying you about in my arms."

Her lips parted. "Oh."

Had he rendered her speechless? Feeling as if he had won the greatest battle of a war, Gill leaned into her, lowering his head. The sweet scent of summery blossoms and Christabella hit him. "But I am glad your ankle is not paining you now nearly as much as it was earlier."

She swallowed, looking suddenly vulnerable and unlike her bold, assured self. "Why is that?"

"Because that means I can kiss you again." And with that, he lowered his head the rest of the way and pressed his lips to hers.

Chapter Eight

$\mathcal{G}$ ILL WAS KISSING her.

In her chamber.

Kissing her madly, passionately, and deliciously.

He had released her hand, and now he cupped her face instead, angling her to him. There was none of the initial hesitance in this kiss. There was only urgency. Full, unadulterated need. A need that echoed within her, in her core. In the wicked place she had read about in *The Book of Love* again and again. The place where he had touched her, only deeper still.

Her flirtation with him was growing dangerous, that much was certain. Dangerous because instead of recalling she had spent the last few years of her life swooning over the notion of being seduced by a rake, all she could think of now was the man kissing her.

The Duke of Coventry.

A man who had never kissed until a few days ago.

She could hardly tell so now, for he was kissing her as if his very life depended upon it, and she was kissing him back with the same desperation. The same fervor. *Heavens*, she would collide with Lady Adele a hundred times over as long as each instance led to this, Gill finding her alone, sitting so near to her she could see every fleck of color in his beautiful eyes and smell his musky citrus scent. Just so she could tangle her fingers in his and chat with him, unencumbered.

She liked this man far, far too much. More than was proper, it was certain. More than she ought to like a gentleman who was not a rake. Not the man she was going to wed.

But he had proposed to her, had he not?

Yes, though it had been abrupt and punctuated by his hasty retreat from the salon that day, he had indeed asked her to marry him. What would she have said, had he not gone? What would she say if he asked her now?

Yes.

No.

Yes.

Certainly not.

Oh, what a dreadful snare to find herself trapped in: a handsome man who was not a rake. A man who had never even taken a woman to his bed. Christabella knew she ought to be ignorant of such matters, but the books she read, along with some light lectures from her sister-in-law Lady Emilia, had given her all the knowledge she needed without a physical demonstration.

Obviously, the physical demonstration would be preferable to words.

Yes, indeed. It would be.

She forgot all the reasons why she should tell Gill to go. Why she should insist upon guarding her reputation. Because kissing him—*good Lord*, his lips on hers—it felt unbearably wonderful and wild. And she could not get enough. She was pulsing and aching everywhere, coming to life. She was a bud blossoming into a hothouse flower.

And she wanted to bloom.

For him.

With him.

His tongue toyed with hers. This was the most delicious

part of kissing, she found—open mouths, tongues writhing—carnal and raw. Or perhaps it was simply the act of kissing Gill, a man who seemed so serious and icy, but who melted for her with such ease.

Her arms were around his neck, and she was clutching him to her, breasts against his chest, tongue meeting his for every thrust. If there were any lingering throbs of pain in her ankle, she forgot them altogether. Her nipples tightened into hard peaks. Her breasts felt full and achy. Her entire body felt as if it had been doused in flame.

In sensual flame.

They were seated alongside each other, making their embrace awkward, the angle of their necks uncomfortable. Instinct guided her. She placed her hands flat on the hard plane of his chest, and gave him a gentle shove.

He ended the kiss, his sky-blue gaze glazed, the obsidian discs of his pupils huge. He blinked, confusion evident on his handsome face.

"I beg your pardon," he began, clearly thinking he needed to apologize.

How wrong he was.

She gave him another tender push, guiding him so that his broad shoulders met with the back of the settee. And then she grasped her skirt in her hands, lifting it to her waist as she straddled his lap. Fortunately, such a position did not require any weight to be distributed upon her ankle.

But who cared about ankles now?

As the already sensitive flesh between her thighs met his breeches and the straining bulge of his manhood beneath them, the breath fled her lungs. She did not think she even knew what an ankle was. Nor would she ever require one again.

All she did require was this. Him.

He was so large, larger even than he had seemed as he sat alongside her. She could see it now, from her vantage point atop him, in a way she had not been able to truly appreciate before. His shoulders were strong and wide. His arms were muscled and long. His chest was hard. His abdomen was flat and lean.

She liked this, being the one in control. She liked being on his lap.

And he liked having her there.

"Belle," he said, his voice low. His countenance was slack with pleasure. His body was taut with need. "What are you doing?"

No one had ever called her Belle before. Christabella, yes. Christabella Mary, also yes. Belle? No. Not anyone. Not until *him*. And she had to admit, she liked it. As much as she liked the sensation of his rock-hard staff beneath her.

She moved over him, relying once more on her instinct. She arched her back, grinding her core upon his breeches-clad member. It was the part of him that should go inside her, if they were lovers. If he were her husband.

He was not.

Nor were they lovers, she reminded herself.

And yet...

How good it felt. *God*, how good it felt. She rocked against him with greater purpose as the need inside her continued to build. Wetness gathered between her thighs. She could feel how slick she was, and she was certain she must be coating his breeches. They were fawn, of fine quality, and she did not care.

All she did care about was seeking the satisfaction only he could give her.

"My God, Belle," he said again, his hands finding her waist.

She realized, quite belatedly, and somehow through the fog of desire permeating her mind, that she had never answered him the first time. He had asked her a question, had he not? Yes, he had. But she could not remember what it had been now. Not with him beneath her, not with her atop him, not with their bodies separated by only the thin barrier of fabric.

Scarcely anything at all.

She found a particularly responsive part of herself, jerking when she brushed herself over his length. Pleasure spiked through her, sharp and unexpected. Wanting more of it, greedy for it, she moved again. His fingers dug into her sides as he gripped her, helping her to move, to angle herself over him.

"Oh, Gill," was all she could manage to say.

The pleasure was too intense. Too overwhelming. She could do nothing but writhe over him, riding him, driving them both ever closer to…something. To the pinnacle she had only read about. To the mindless, sated bliss. She wanted that. He wanted that. She knew it without having to ask.

But then, his fingers somehow found their way beneath her skirts. And they found, unerringly, the part of her that was hungriest. She cried out and slammed her mouth down on his.

HE HAD ONLY intended to come here to inquire after her ankle. To reassure himself she was not suffering from too much pain. But somehow, in spite of all his good intentions, Christabella was in his lap, and his hand was beneath her gown. She had just been riding his cock through his breeches, and the falls of them were kissed with her dew.

His fingers explored. Parted her. She was slick and hot. A dream. Familiar, too. His, all his. He circled her pearl with his forefinger, exerting more pressure than he had the last time. There was no hesitance in him now. Only hunger. He learned her, listening to the sweet hitches in her breath that told him when she liked what he did. To the throaty cries and the jerk of her hips that told him she wanted more.

And he gave her more.

He wanted to make her spend. Wanted to feel her lose herself. Wanted to watch as pleasure rushed over her and she became helpless and mindless. Their lips met once more and clung, this kiss more passionate even than all the others that came before. Although it had been mere hours since their sultry interlude in the writing room, he was on fire for her.

His entire body vibrated with the need to be one with her. A need he could not fulfill, a desire he could not yet quench. Because she was not his wife. She had not even agreed to marry him yet. The reminder should have quelled some of the lust raging inside him. It should have made him pluck her off his lap and put some necessary distance between them.

But he did not. Because she brought him to life in a way he had never imagined possible. She made him believe, for the first time, that happiness would not forever hover beyond his reach. That he was stronger than the affliction which had chased him all his life.

Faster and faster he worked over the swollen bud. His hand was coated in the evidence of her desire. She moved with him, undulating her hips and thrusting over him in a delicious rhythm. Their kiss turned voracious. He was almost on the edge himself, his cock aching after the way she had moved over him. His ballocks were drawn tight, white-hot desire licking down his spine.

She was ready.

Gill did not know how he knew, for he was a novice at pleasuring a woman. Perhaps it was the way she sped up. Or the way she cried out into his mouth. Or the way she slammed her cunny against him frantically, as if they could become one with this single act alone.

He circled her pearl, rubbing harder.

Until she stiffened, her body shuddering. She moaned. It was the most erotic sound he had ever heard in his bloody life. He ate up that moan. Ate up her kiss. Her lips. Continued pleasuring her even as need hummed through him, threatening to make him lose control.

She never stopped kissing him, rocking into his touch. Her cunny was even wetter now than it had been before. Ready. He wondered what it would feel like to slide deep inside her. Inside her heat, her wetness. It would be bliss, he had no doubt. The sort that would tear him asunder.

And he could not wait.

But he would not breach her, not until she was his in truth. As badly as he longed to further explore her, he would not. Not even with his fingers. She would be his wife before he would go that far, he vowed it.

Which reminded him.

He tore his mouth from hers and drank in the sight of her. Christabella's lips were swollen, her jaw slack, eyes closed. She was flushed and disheveled and delicious. He had done that to her. And he loved it.

Her eyes fluttered open. Her gaze met his, the flush on her cheeks deepening to a shade that rivaled her bold locks.

"Gill," she breathed.

There was one question on his mind.

"Will you marry me?" he asked for the second time in as many days.

"Marry you," she repeated, her brow furrowing.

Devil take it. Why did she sound so hesitant?

The affliction was beating down on him. Making his chest seize. But this time, there was no easy means of escape. She was still sprawled on his lap, his hand was still up her skirts, nestled in the wicked warmth of her cunny, and even if movement had been possible, he was determined not to flee this time.

He removed his hand with the greatest reluctance, for proposing whilst his hand was buried between her thighs hardly seemed the gentlemanly thing to do. "Yes. I am in need of a wife. You are unwed. I...like you."

Curse it, what was the matter with him? Had a worse proposal ever been made to a lady? His heart was pounding. A prickle started on his skin.

"I like you too," she told him, removing herself from his lap and rearranging the fall of her gown as she maneuvered herself back to his side. "But I am not ready to marry just yet."

She was not ready to marry, and yet she had just allowed him to make indecent advances. Anger sliced through him, replacing the desire.

"You are not ready to marry?" It was his return to echo her words. "Is it because there is another?"

"Not precisely." She fidgeted with her gown, avoiding his gaze.

He did not like the sound of that.

A possessive surge of jealousy shot through him next. He clenched his fists impotently at his sides. "Who is he?"

"There is no one else I wish to marry, Gill," she said, looking up at last. "Not yet."

His brows snapped together. "There is no one else you wish to marry, but neither do you wish to marry me, despite allowing me to touch your cunny and make you come."

She flinched, perhaps from the vehemence of his words,

which startled even him. "There is no need to be crude."

He shot to his feet, anger rising like a tide within him. Anger at himself. Anger at her. "I was not being crude, madam. I was being honest. Brutally so. Did you not just climb atop my lap, kiss me, and find pleasure?"

She paled, looking as if he had struck her.

He felt as if he had.

What a cad he was. Yes, she had done those things. But there was no call to make her feel shame for them, merely because she had rejected his suit. He had to leave before he said something else. Something worse.

He offered her a stiff bow. "Good day, Miss Winter."

Without waiting for her response, he turned and stalked from her chamber.

Chapter Nine

CHRISTABELLA SPENT THE next day in a sea of misery, favoring her ankle and attempting to stifle her yawns. She had not been able to sleep, and the reason had nothing to do with the slight twinge in her ankle whenever she'd shifted in her bed. Rather, it had been the expression on Gill's face when she had turned down his proposal of marriage.

He had been hurt.

She had hurt him.

And after he had just given her the most intense pleasure she had ever known.

It had not been her intention to wound him. His proposal had taken her by surprise. Also, since he had only asked her to marry him on two instances, both of which occurred in the wake of his hand between her legs, she was partially afraid he was being guided by lust rather than other motives.

"Christabella?"

Pru's voice interrupted her thoughts, reminding her she was surrounded by her sisters whilst she gathered wool. They had all congregated in one chamber to ready themselves for dinner that evening. And she had no wish for her ever-perceptive sisters to know what was troubling her. If she had to explain, she would have to mention the shocking lapse of propriety in which she had engaged, along with the liberties she had allowed...

Liberties that made her heart pound and desire flare to life deep in her core once more. She had never kissed a rake, but she was certain not even the wickedest rake in the realm's kiss could compare to Gill's. He kissed her as if he wanted to brand her with his lips, as if he wanted to keep her in his arms forever.

Because he did.

He wanted to marry her.

Blast.

She forced a smile to her lips and attempted to look nonchalant as her sisters watched her, their expressions expectant. "Yes, dearest sister?"

"I asked you how your ankle is feeling," Pru said pointedly. "Are you sure you are well? You seem distracted this evening."

"The Duke of Coventry proposed," she blurted. "I declined."

"He did?" Pru's brows rose. "You did?"

"When?" Eugie and Bea asked.

"Why?" Bea added. "Why would you refuse him, I mean to say. Not why would he propose to you. Clearly, he would propose to you because you are beautiful and the duke knows a wonderfully intelligent, kindhearted lady when he sees one."

"Did he write his proposal in a letter?" Grace queried dryly, cutting through sweet Bea's kindness in her own way.

Christabella sighed. So much for wishing to keep the information to herself. Not ten minutes into being surrounded by her beloved sisters, and she was telling them all her secrets. As one did with one's sisters.

"Yesterday," she admitted, answering Eugie and Bea's questions first.

"Before or after your injury?" Pru asked shrewdly.

"Both." The instant the word left her, she winced.

All her sisters began chattering at once.

"How many times has he proposed?"

"Where you alone with him?"

"Has he ruined you?"

"Did he actually speak?"

Christabella blinked as she tried to make sense of which sister had asked what question. "He has proposed twice, Pru. And yes, Bea, I was alone with him. No, Eugie, he has not ruined me. And Grace, Coventry is fully capable of speaking. Indeed, he speaks quite eloquently when he wishes. He simply struggles in gatherings. His struggles were no match for me, however. I made my way through them with tickling, snowballs, and good sense."

Also, kissing.

She refrained from mentioning that last bit.

And then she realized her sisters were all eying her in a similar fashion.

Her cheeks went hot. "Why are you looking at me thus?"

"Of course it would be you." Grace was the first to speak, shaking her head.

"What do you mean?" she demanded, the tips of her ears feeling quite hot by now. "Of course what would be me?"

"Surely you can see the irony," Grace said gently. "You are the sister who, of us all, has vowed to snare a rake. And yet, you have lost your heart to a man who scarcely even speaks, let alone charms anyone."

He had charmed her.

With his mouth.

And his strong arms.

His sparkling blue eyes.

His smile.

His laughter.

His knowing fingers…

Drat. What was she thinking? She chased all thoughts of Gill from her mind, struggling to maintain her ability to reason.

"And a rake I shall yet ensnare," she declared, perturbed that her voice did not hold nearly as much conviction as it ought.

That it sounded instead quite hollow. Uncertain, even.

"Of course you shall." Grace rolled her eyes in typical Grace fashion.

Irritation sparked through her. "Yes, I shall. Do you doubt me?"

"Do not be foolish," Pru cautioned. "Rakes are not all they seem to be."

"But are you not marrying Lord Ashley, one of the wickedest rakes in all London?" Christabella could not help but to ask.

After all, Pru had just been discovered in a most compromising situation with Lord Ashley. By a servant, no less. Their brother Dev had been enraged, and he was demanding Pru marry Lord Ashley as a result.

"I have no choice in the matter," Pru said.

"You are in love, however," Bea offered.

"Lord Ashley has been chasing you all over Abingdon House since his arrival," Grace added.

"He does seem to have eyes only for you," Eugie added to Pru, which was a surprise, for she was ordinarily quite jaded when it came to noblemen.

Christabella supposed falling in love with her betrothed, the Earl of Hertford, had changed all that for her sister. Love seemed to change everything. She stared at her sisters, all of them preparing to wed. Grace had lost her heart to Lord Aylesford somehow along the way, and the two of them were now betrothed in truth. Even Pru, who seemed shocked by the harried nature of the decision involving herself, looked, beneath it all, happy.

Contented.

That was how they all looked. In love. About to marry men who would make them deliriously happy.

An unwanted spear of envy pricked her. She longed for that same happiness. To be assured of love. Of a husband who loved her. For over the course of the last few weeks of the house party, Christabella had watched her sisters fall in love. She had watched their future husbands looking upon them with unreserved affection, as if they were the only ladies in a chamber.

And what did she have? Not the grand passion she had always been longing for, certainly.

Or did she?

"We are not speaking of me, however," Pru interrupted, her maternal instinct on full display. "We are speaking of Christabella and the Duke of Coventry."

"And his many proposals," Grace added with a raised brow, pinning her with a probing look.

"It was only two," she defended.

"Two proposals is rather unusual," Bea pointed out.

"It suggests strong emotions," Eugie said.

Christabella exhaled on a long sigh. "It suggests confusion. I am the first lady he has ever kissed."

"You have kissed him?" Grace asked, brows going skyward. "How many times?"

More times than she could count.

All those kisses came flooding back to her now, along with a rush of tangled-up emotions. His mouth on hers…it was bliss. She wanted it again. What did that mean?

She swallowed, contemplating her response. About to lie.

"More times than she cares to admit," answered Bea on

her behalf.

Her youngest sister was wise beyond her years. But Christabella glared at her all the same. "How do you know?"

"Your expression," Eugie answered definitively.

"You look guilty," Pru observed.

"Guiltier than whom? Than any of the rest of you?" she could not help but to counter. She was feeling defensive, yes. But being examined by her sisters had not been her intention this evening. Indeed, she had meant to hold her tongue. To say nothing.

To…

What?

To forget Gill had ever kissed her? To forget he had turned her world asunder each time he touched her? To forget the mindless bliss he had visited upon her with his fingers alone?

How could she forget any of that? Moreover, how could she forget him?

The answer seemed glaring, if unwanted.

She could not.

But he was not what she wanted. He was not a rake. He had not declared his love for her in charming and effusive fashion. He had not led her into a darkened chamber and ravished her.

The only problem with all that logic was that she was beginning to fear those were all just childish fancies. The longings of a girl who had never before been swept away by a man before her rather than a man between the pages of a book.

Her sisters were gaping at her in the wake of her outburst.

Christabella raised her fingertips to her cheek and discovered the reason why as she touched the wet trails of her tears. She was weeping. Weeping and miserable and confused. So horribly, irrevocably confused.

"You are in love with him," Bea declared.

"Nay," she denied. "I am not."

"Do you want to kiss him again?" Grace asked. "Is he all you can think of, even when you close your eyes to sleep at night?"

Yes.

She clamped her lips tight.

"Does being in his arms make you feel as if you have come home?" Eugie added next.

She thought of his citrus and musk scent, his long, strong arms. Thought of how effortlessly he had scooped her into his arms. Thought of clinging to him. Of his embrace.

"It is pleasant enough," she allowed grudgingly.

Which was, of course, a wretched lie.

Being in Gill's arms was *everything*.

"Is he the one you continually find yourself drawn to, even when it goes against everything within you, all your reason, your common sense, your best intentions otherwise?" Pru added, her tone contemplative.

Perhaps she was thinking of her own circumstances.

Christabella bit her lip, pondering her sister's question. The answer was as plain as the nose upon her face. Of course she was drawn to Gill. It had not happened intentionally. But it had happened quickly. With shocking speed. One day, she had thought him frigid as an icicle, and the next he had been the flame.

"I…" She struggled to make sense of her emotions, to give voice to what she was feeling inside, and failed.

But as it turned out, she did not require eloquence. She had sisters, and they read her heart. Better, it would seem, than she had.

They surrounded her in the next moment, until she stood

in the center of their circle. Their arms were entwined in one endless hug.

"Winter hug," they said.

Her heart warmed, in spite of her confusion. How she loved her sisters. They were all so different from each other. But they were the same in one respect: they loved each other and they were fiercely protective of one another. They all understood that they were Winters. For so long, it had been them against the rest of the world.

Now, their world was growing larger.

"Christabella?" Pru asked.

"Yes?" she ventured, eyes still closed tight.

"The next time he asks you to marry him, accept," Bea counseled.

"You are in love," Grace added.

"And, unless we are all mistaken, which never happens," Eugie said, "he is in love with you."

"As he ought to be." Pru pressed a kiss to her forehead, half-sisterly, half-maternal. "Any man would be fortunate to have you as his wife."

"The same can be said of you," she told her sisters. "Of all of you."

"It is a bloody good thing you added the rest of us," Grace said. "Else I may have had to resort to pulling hair."

All the sisters dissolved into a fit of giggles.

When she caught her breath again, Christabella hugged the circle of her sisters to her tightly. "How do I know if I am in love with him? Or for that matter, how do I know if he is in love with me?"

"You will know it in your heart," Eugie said.

And that was precisely what Christabella was afraid of.

❄

GILL TOOK ONE look at his brother's countenance, and he knew what Ash was about to say.

"You have fallen in love with Miss Prudence Winter," he pronounced.

Ash's shoulders went stiff, a frown drawing his brows together. "How did you know?"

There was only one reason why Ash would come dashing to his chamber whilst he readied for dinner. And only one reason why his brother would look so concerned and yet elated, all at once. He did his damnedest not to feel bitter about the fact that he had been right all along in his supposition that if one of them could be happy, it would be Ash.

Never Gill.

"You are my brother," he forced himself to say by way of explanation.

"How long have you known?" Ash demanded, a sharp edge of outrage inherent in his voice.

"Since our arrival here." Gill tied a knot in his cravat himself, since he had already dismissed his valet, Martin to enable him to have this conversation with his brother sans audience.

"Since our arrival," Ash repeated, looking shocked. "But what of the wager? You told me you wanted to make Pru your duchess."

"I told you I wanted to find my duchess here, and that I was willing to accept your aid," he explained. "We both know I am as useless as a ham when it comes to the fairer sex. You, however, were the one who suggested Miss Prudence."

And he was still as useless as a ham.

He could make Miss Christabella come, but he could not make her agree to be his duchess.

"I was not the one who suggested it," his brother denied.

"You could not stop staring at her from the moment you

first saw her," he countered. "I had hoped the two of you might suit. You simply needed the proper motivation. A wager seemed just the thing."

"The devil. You mean to tell me that this whole time, whilst I thought I was helping you to find a bride, *you*, my virginal, saintly brother, were actually helping *me* to acquire a bride?"

Gill grinned at that. Grimly, of course. Because he was no longer as virginal as he had once been. And he was certainly not saintly. "Yes."

"Confound it, Gill." Ash's outrage had returned. "Have you any idea how guilty I felt this last fortnight, believing I was lusting over the woman you wanted to make your duchess?"

The very notion of Ash lusting over Christabella— regardless of how much he loved his brother—made Gill long to do violence.

"You ought to have done," he told Ash. "And if you had indeed been lusting after the woman I want to make my duchess, I would have planted you a facer."

"The woman you want to make your duchess?" His brother's gaze narrowed. "Are you saying there *is* someone else you want to wed in attendance at this house party?"

"There may be," he hedged, mostly because he had no wish to reveal the full extent of his failure to his brother, who had never met a lady he could not charm out of her gown.

But Ash was no fool. "Not the hellion?"

His back stiffened at his brother's insulting sobriquet for Christabella. She was wild, yes. And bold, no doubt. But she was his, *damn it*, and he felt deuced protective of her.

No, she is not yours, taunted a voice inside him.

God's truth. She did not want to marry him. Unless he could find sufficient means of persuasion.

He busied himself with tying his cravat, trying to distract himself from the misery of her rejection and his subsequent withdrawal. "I have no notion of whom you are speaking. I do trust, however, that you would not refer to your future wife's sister in such terms."

"Who said I am marrying Pru?" Ash asked.

He raised a brow at his brother. "*You*. You have never once professed your love for a female to me. And from what I gather, the number of females with whom you have been on intimate terms is legion."

"I am not proud of the manner in which I have lived my life," Ash said, his tone as stiff as his bearing. "I have spent years chasing nothing but pleasure, telling myself it was what led to happiness. But I have discovered, quite belatedly, just how wrong I was. I do not deserve Pru, that much is certain. But I want to marry her."

He knew the feeling. Well, part of the feeling. He had not spent his life chasing pleasure, but rather duty. And an attempt to avoid most social interaction. Christabella had made him realize he was stronger than he had believed. That perhaps with time and motivation, he could at least control his affliction, if not banish it altogether.

She had filled him with hope.

Until she struck it down.

Still, this was not about him and Christabella. Rather, this was about the brother he loved finding happiness at last, a happiness which he so richly deserved. "I am glad you have finally seen what has been plain enough to me. When will the betrothal be announced?"

"This evening," Ash said, shocking him.

Too damned bad that Miss Prudence's sister was not so hasty in her decision. And that she had an aversion to telling him *yes* unless it came to kisses and touching.

"Remarkably quick of you, Ash," he pointed out, hating himself for the bitterness in his tone.

He should be happy for his brother.

And he was.

But for the first time, he also wanted happiness for himself. And he was beginning to fear the way he felt about Miss Christabella Winter could only be described in one fashion. In a fashion which involved a four-letter word that rhymed with dove.

"Yes, well." Ash fiddled with his cravat, looking suddenly shamefaced. "I may have compromised Pru."

"You *may have* compromised her, or you *did*?" Gill asked.

It would seem they had both been acting the scoundrel this house party. Who would have believed it? Not him. *Bloody hell*, what was the matter with them? Perhaps they were more their father's sons than either of them had realized.

"I did," Ash admitted with a grimace. "It was unintentional, I swear it, and nothing untoward occurred. Well, actually, it did, but that was before we were discovered."

Sadly, his brother's words resonated, for they were all too familiar.

"Nothing you are saying is reassuring me," Gill said as it occurred to him that both he and Ash had compromised Winter sisters at the same house party. Perhaps even on the same day.

Lord God have mercy upon them.

"It is...complicated," Ash told him. "Suffice it to say, the lady took a fall in the snow, and I was left with no recourse but to help her disrobe so her garments would dry."

Was it wrong of him that for a moment he wished something similar had befallen himself and Christabella? A well-timed fall in the snow, the necessity of removing a wet gown...

Yes, he told himself. It was wrong of him to think. Such thoughts ought to be beneath him.

What a shame they are not, whispered a hideous voice within.

A voice he promptly quashed as he pinned his brother with a look of disapproval. "Ash. Tell me you did not seduce her."

"I did not seduce her," Ash said quickly before raking a hand through his hair. "That is the truth. At least, not in the moment when we were discovered. But never mind that. We were in the false ruins, and my garments were quite sodden as well. I had no recourse but to join her beneath the fur, and then we—"

"Bloody hell, Ash!" Gill burst out. "Did you have to tup the sister of the woman I want to make my wife? Could you not have waited until the damned wedding night?"

"We fell asleep!" Ash was indignant until the remainder of Gill's words apparently hit him, and his expression changed entirely, as if he were just fully grasping the situation for the first time. "The woman you want to make your wife? You *do* want to marry the hellion."

"She is not a hellion," he felt compelled to defend this time around.

She was beautiful and seductive. Silly and wonderful. She threw snowballs at him and tickled him. She kissed him. She made him long for her desperately.

He had spent most of his life locked away from feeling and emotion, much the way his father had locked him in that chamber so long ago. He did not even know if it was possible for him to love a woman. He loved his brother, but that was not the same. They shared blood and a haunted past. They were all each other had.

Christabella, however…she was different.

Ash started laughing then. Uncontrollably. He carried on until his maniacal laughter produced tears in his eyes and he was forced to withdraw a handkerchief from his coat and dab at his eyes.

Gill was just about to ask his brother if he was feeling well when Ash spoke again at last. "What a pair we are. Perhaps I was right when I said there is something in the food here. A poison that rots men's minds and makes them more susceptible to matchmaking."

There was a poison afoot indeed, and Gill was fairly certain what it was, much to his dismay.

"The poison is love," he decided, his grim mood returning.

For what could love be but a poison if it existed only as a source of torment? If a man found the woman he wanted to marry and she told him no?

Twice, curse it.

"But is love a poison, or is it a cure?" Ash stroked his jaw as he appeared to contemplate the question himself. "It seems one could argue either way."

Gill sighed. The way he felt when he was with Christabella—if it was indeed love—more than made up for the suffering. And yet knowing he may have lost his heart to her whilst there remained the very real possibility she had only been flirting with him and kissing him out of boredom or—worse—curiosity, stung.

"One could, indeed," he finally allowed reluctantly.

He and Ash were silent for a moment, a tacit acknowledgment passing between them.

"Let us hope it is a cure," Ash decided.

Gill was certain it was the poison. It sure as hell felt that way now, festering inside his gut, threatening to be his undoing.

"She has refused me," he blurted, before he could think better of the admission.

"The hellion?" Ash frowned.

"Devil take it, her name is Christabella," Gill snapped, irritated by his brother's continued insistence upon referring to her thus.

"Steady, brother." Ash flashed him a grin. "I was attempting to make a sally."

"Poorly timed," he muttered, fiddling with the knot he had fastened in his cravat.

Martin had a much more adept hand than he did when it came to such matters. But Martin also enjoyed gossiping below stairs. And Gill had no wish for his or his brother's romantic endeavors at this house party to become fodder for every lady's maid and valet in Abingdon House.

"Forgive me." Ash paused, cocking his head and considering Gill in a way that made him long to squirm. "You have offered for her hand, then?"

"Twice," he admitted, making certain to omit the full details.

"Have you been sneaking about with her, you scoundrel?" Ash asked, his grin deepening.

"Not sneaking." His ears were hot. His cravat was too damned tight. "Very well, one of the occasions was a planned meeting. The others, however, were happenstance. Except for when I went to her chamber…"

Ash shook his head, as if he could not believe his ears. "Bloody hell, Gill. You went to her chamber? And here you were giving me hell about Pru, whilst you have been sneaking about in chambers. Now that you mention it, sneaking about in chambers with Pru may be just the thing…"

"She had injured her ankle, and I wished to make certain she was not in pain," he defended himself, even though the words rang hollow to his own ears.

In truth, he could have waited. There had been no reason to seek her out. He could have inquired after her the next morning, at breakfast. He could have stayed far, far away from her, damn it.

But he had not.

Because he was drawn to her. Because he could not resist her.

"I feel as if I ought to lecture you on the importance of observing the proprieties," Ash said then. "This is the devil of a thing. I never supposed you would be acting the rogue."

Had he been acting the rogue? The thought gave him pause.

"I am not acting the rogue," he decided. "I am attempting to make her my duchess."

"And yet the lady is not keen," Ash mused, stroking his jaw. "I thought most ladies wanted nothing more than to snare a coronet until I met Pru. These Winter ladies are a law unto themselves, Gill. One must proceed with caution. And a battle plan. Tell me, what did you say to her when you asked her to marry you?"

He thought back to his awkward proposal and grimaced as his own words returned to him.

I am in need of a wife. You are unwed. I...like you.

"I told her I liked her," he said. "And she was unwed."

Ash nodded. "Decent. And?"

"And that was all."

Ash whistled. "Ah, I begin to see the problem."

He stiffened. "Here now, just because you have bedded half the ladies in London does not mean you know how to procure a wife any better than I do."

"And yet, I am a betrothed man whilst you are not," pointed out his cursed brother, looking and sounding equally smug.

"Because you have ruined Miss Prudence, and you have been caught doing it," he could not help but to point out.

"But she has agreed to the marriage, whilst the hellion has not."

His hands balled into impotent fists as his sides. "If you call her that one more time, Ash, by God, I will be forced to plant you a facer after all."

Ash laughed, the cheeky scoundrel. "Forgive me. I never thought I would see the day when my brother fell in love, and I must admit it is devilishly entertaining."

"Go to hell," he grumbled, aware he was flushing now, quite like a callow youth.

Which in some ways, he still was.

"But as much fun as it is to watch you squirm, my true aim is to assist you," Ash continued. "Tell me, what did Miss Christabella say when you asked her to marry you?"

On which occasion?

Ballocks. He truly was pathetic, was he not?

"She told me she likes me," he said, "but that she is not ready to marry just yet."

"Intriguing." Ash was still stroking his jaw, as if he were pondering.

Gill waited for his brother to say something, but his impatience got the better of him. "Well? Have you nothing to offer?"

"Have you kissed her?"

His cheeks went hotter. "Yes."

"And she responded?" Ash pressed.

He thought of Christabella's sweet, husky sounds. Her tongue in his mouth. The way she had climbed into his lap and changed his entire world. The slick heat of her cunny...

Blast. He could not continue in that vein of thought

112

whilst his brother stood there.

"She responded," he gritted.

Ash gave him a look of approval and clapped him on the shoulder. "Excellent, brother. It sounds as if the lady requires further persuasion."

He had already kissed her. Often and prodigiously. Made her spend. Proposed to her.

What other means of persuasion existed? As a neophyte, he was lost.

"What do you have in mind?" he asked his brother.

Ash's countenance turned contemplative. "I believe it is past time you made Miss Christabella come to you. A gentleman cannot do all the chasing, you see. Sometimes, the lady must see the error of her ways. If she has yet to realize what her heart is telling her, you must help in the oldest fashion there is."

"Which is?" he prodded.

Ash flashed yet another devilish grin. "Jealousy."

That would never work.

"Excellent idea if I were the sort of man capable of wooing the females in my presence." He paused, thinking of his cursed affliction. "The only lady I want to speak with or court is Belle."

"Belle?" Ash's lips twitched as if he were attempting to stifle laughter.

He glared. "I cannot make her jealous, even if I wished to, which I do not. Have you nothing else to suggest? If so, run along so I can recall Martin to fix my cravat."

His brother appeared to be contemplating once more, apparently running through his vast experience as a practiced wooer of the fairer sex for a winning strategy.

At last, a Machiavellian smile dawned on Ash's countenance. "I believe I have just the thing."

Chapter Ten

*T*HERE WAS NO sign of Gill.

Christabella tried to tell herself his absence did not concern her. She tried to tell herself staying away from him was truly for the best anyway. Distance and separation were what they required. All the better to clear her mind.

To convince herself that her sisters were wrong.

That she was not in love with the Duke of Coventry.

That it did not bother her one whit that here she was in the vast drawing room once more, surrounded by the house party guests, prepared to partake in yet another entertainment without him.

But it did.

She seated herself at Pru's side, fidgeting with her skirts, as their sister-in-law announced the afternoon's distraction would be charades.

For the third time.

She cast a sidelong glance at her sister whilst Lady Emilia spoke, thinking Pru looked irritatingly happy. Pru and Lord Ashley were making eyes at each other across the drawing room, acting as if they were the only two people in the chamber.

Love.

It was ridiculously irritating.

How had she ever imagined it would be the answer to all

her problems?

"Have you inquired after Coventry with Lord Ashley?" she whispered to her sister, although she had promised herself she would not ask again.

She had already asked at least half a dozen times, and on each occasion, Pru gave her the same noncommittal response. The duke was apparently ill. And though she did not want to worry over him, Christabella could not help it. She *was* worried.

It had been an entire day, after all.

"Coventry is still indisposed," Pru murmured back without bothering to sever her eye contact with her betrothed. "Something about a lung infection, I believe."

A lung infection? This was news to Christabella. Her stomach clenched.

"Lung infections can be quite serious," she fretted aloud.

"Hmm?" Pru asked, her attention still pinned upon Gill's brother.

Why had Christabella ever imagined a rake would be the sort of man to turn her head and win her heart, anyway? Lord Ashley was handsome enough, but there was something about Gill's lack of seductive polish she could not resist. He was earnest. And his kisses were... Well, she could not fathom a rake's could compare.

But what manner of illness would force him to remain in his chamber for the last remaining days of the house party? She knew he did not particularly care for socializing and drawing room games, but with Christmastide upon them and the party about to come to an end, Christabella was beginning to worry she would not even see him again before he departed.

The thought left her with a hollow ache she could not shake. As did the notion of him abed, suffering, all alone.

"Has his condition improved?" she prodded her sister.

After all, Pru's betrothed was Gill's own brother. Who better to ask?

Christabella herself did not yet feel comfortable enough with Lord Ashley to make demands of him. When he was officially her brother, she had no doubt that would change.

"Has his inclination moved?" Pru asked, at last sparing Christabella a glance. A hasty glance, before returning to her previous task of making lovesick eyes at Lord Ashley. "What nonsense are you spouting now, Christabella?"

"Have you not listened to a word I have spoken?" she demanded, careful to keep her voice low lest others overhear her outrage. "That is not at all what I said. Little wonder you think it nonsensical."

"I did not think it made much sense, but in my defense, you are often spouting about some romanticism or other, darling," Pru told her.

"Would you kindly direct your attention to me whilst I am speaking with you?" she demanded, her dudgeon now quite high. "Lord Ashley is not the only person in this chamber, you know. I am your sister, and I am worried about the state of your future brother-in-law's health. Indeed, one might think you could show a bit more concern. Do you not care for Coventry at all?"

"Of course I care for him." She shot Christabella an irritated look at last. "He is not on his deathbed, Christabella. As I understand it, he is resting and shall recover quite nicely. There is nothing to fret over."

How wrong Pru was.

There was *everything* to fret over.

But Christabella clamped her lips shut and turned her attention to the game. Lady Fawkesbury was in the midst of attempting to demonstrate something that rather resembled a swan. But the entertainment did not distract her sufficiently.

Even when her spirits were not weighed down by worry, and on the best of days, Christabella found charades a tedious pastime indeed. She far preferred Snapdragon, which involved fishing raisins out of a bowl of burning brandy with one's bare fingers.

Flames made things ever so much more interesting.

But that was neither here nor there.

Christabella tapped her foot. Then she fidgeted upon the settee. She plucked at the drapery of her gown. She bit her lip. She tried, once more, to remember that she had not wanted to marry Gill. She had turned down his proposal twice, after all. It was only her sisters who believed she had lost her heart to him, who had convinced her that perhaps she ought to marry him after all. Likely, they were all wrong. Their incorrect suppositions were a natural effect of having lost their hearts to their own respective future husbands.

"Pru," she tried again, irritated with herself for speaking and yet unable to bite her tongue. "Has he mentioned me?"

Her sister sent her another look, this one markedly sympathetic. "If he did, Ash did not say so. But I am certain he holds you in highest esteem. Else why would he want you for his wife?"

But *did* he want her for his wife? His proposals, even when he had offered them, had all been in the wake of intense sensual encounters between the two of them. Moreover, did she want him as her husband? Just when she had begun to consider the notion she had been wrong, all these years, about what she truly wanted, Gill had grown ill and disappeared.

Before she could think better of it, she blurted out her greatest fear, aside from her worries over his health. "What if he no longer wants me as his wife?"

"He would be a fool to change his mind," Pru reassured her softly, giving her knee a gentle pat. "But there is only one person who can give you the answers you seek, my dear. And that is Coventry himself."

Yes, it was Coventry alone who could tell her, was it not? Which meant there was only one means by which she could have the answers she sought. The answer to just how ill he was. And the answer to how he felt about her and how she felt about him.

She shot to her feet, ignoring the startled glances from the rest of the company. Ignoring, too, her sister's protest.

Her mind was made up.

She was going to find Gill's bedchamber.

And she was going to trespass.

She was going to force her way inside and see for herself what state he was in. One way or another.

Her feet started moving. And that quickly, she was gone from the drawing room. A world away from the revelers within. Charades was the last thing on her mind now. As was propriety.

She needed answers, and she needed them now.

CHRISTABELLA WAS NOT going to come.

Gill stood at the window of his bedchamber, the one which overlooked the immense, snow-encrusted lawns of Abingdon Hall's sprawling park, along with the serpentine lake that cut through it. The day was bright, thanks to the reflective nature of the snow. It was also cold. Icy air radiated from the glass panes, kissing his lips.

It was not the kiss he wanted, that much was certain. Nor was it the kiss he longed for, the kiss that kept him awake late at night.

That kiss, it was becoming more apparent, would never

again be his. He leaned his forehead against the cool pane, relishing the chill, along with the draught of winter's wind as a blustery gust sent snow rushing from the roof of the centuries' old manor house.

It looked as if it were snowing all over again. Wisps of snow glistened in the sunlight, fleeting and elusive in its beauty. Making him think—as if his damned mind had ever strayed in the course of the last day—once more of her.

Devil take Ash and his stupid notions.

Feigning an illness and hiding himself away in his chamber had not done one whit of good. It had been an entire day.

A whole. Bloody. Day.

And whilst Gill did not mind hiding himself away from his fellow revelers and taking a much-needed respite from an endless barrage of faces, there was one face he missed. One face he longed for. One woman he was beginning to fear he may have lost forever.

If he had ever had her.

What would a bold, gorgeous lady like Christabella Winter want with a husk of a man who could not even manage to form coherent sentences in large gatherings of people? Nothing, as was blatantly apparent by her lack of attempt to seek him out.

Every time he had asked Ash if Christabella had inquired after him, Ash had been gentle in his reassurance that he had no doubt she would. At some point.

At some point.

By God, at this rate of speed, Gill would have to closet himself in the east wing of Abingdon House for the rest of his natural life before Miss Christabella Winter would come looking for him. Or to worry over his health. He ought to be ashamed of himself for even supposing someone like her could ever deign to be the wife of a man like him. A man who was still the same scared lad, in some ways, that his bastard of a father had locked inside that windowless room.

All these years later, and the fear still chased him.

He did not deserve a woman like her, that was for certain.

The door clicked open behind him, but he did not bother to turn. More than likely, it was his valet Martin, arriving with a tray of some sort. When one kept to one's rooms, the hours of the day all bled hopelessly together. It could be dinner for all he knew. His stomach certainly had no wish for sustenance.

"Leave it on the table, if you please, Martin," he directed, still staring morosely out the window. In search of answers. In search of himself.

His valet did not respond. There was the sound of the door closing once more, then hushed footfalls. Footfalls which did not sound at all like his lumbering manservant, who—whilst an adroit hand at tying knots—was incapable of moving anywhere without stomping thanks to his massive size. Rather, they sounded like—

"Gill."

His name, nothing more.

In her voice.

He jerked from the window and spun about, half convincing himself he had imagined her calling his name. The sight of her, standing in the center of the chamber, ethereally beautiful in an ivory gown, stole his breath and his voice both.

She had come.

He swallowed, forgetting entirely that he was supposed to be ill. "Belle."

His sobriquet for her. Somehow, it emerged of its own accord, natural and right although he knew he had no claims upon her. He was more aware of that fact than ever as he faced her now, itching to draw her into his arms.

Her brow was furrowed, her gaze searching his. "How are you?"

"Bloody dreadful," he answered honestly.

Going a day without her had been pure, unadulterated hell. He had been trapped in a web of his own making, in a chamber with windows and sunlight but no Christabella, which was its own sort of pain.

"I know I should not be here," she said, wringing her hands, almost as if she were not certain where to go or what to do.

"You should not," he agreed. "If you are discovered here, you will be ruined. Since you have already expressed your marked disinterest in marrying me, I suggest you go."

His words emerged with a bitterness he regretted the moment they were spoken. For they hung in the air between them, vibrating like a remonstration.

"Do you want me to go?" she asked, her gaze searching his.

Of course he did not. She was finally precisely where he wanted her, within his reach. And yet, he could not bring himself to do any of the things he had told himself he must to win her. The thought of making himself vulnerable to her made him want to retch.

"Why have you come?" he asked instead.

"I could not stay away." Her voice was soft. So soft, he had to strain to hear her. "I needed to see for myself just how ill you were."

Her concern filled him with warmth. But the trepidation lingered, tightening into a knot in his gut. Perhaps she cared for him, but that did not mean she wished to marry him any more now than she had on the previous two occasions when he had posed the question.

He cleared his throat, feeling deuced awkward, and said nothing.

They each stood rooted to their respective spots, she in the middle of his chamber, and he on the periphery. It all seemed somehow symbolic. Christabella Winter was the life of a chamber. He was, as she had rightly pointed out, frigid as an icicle while she was the flame.

Despite hoping she would come to him, now that she finally had, he could not help but think perhaps a marriage between them would be a mistake. Could he ever be what she needed?

"Will you not say anything?" she asked.

He wanted to speak, but the affliction had returned with a vengeance. It settled in his throat, choking him.

"Very well. If you shall not, then I will." She came nearer at last, bringing with her the scent of summer and sunshine and delicious temptation. "I am sorry about what happened in my chamber that day."

At last, his voice returned. "As am I. What I said to you was unpardonable, and for that I must offer you my most sincere apologies."

He had been an utter blackguard, lashing out at her, and he knew it. Feeling emotions was new for him. Everything about Christabella was new to him, in fact.

"I accept your apologies on one condition." She took another step closer to him.

Until she was within touching distance.

He had to exercise all his restraint to keep from taking her into his arms as everything within him so desperately wanted. For he could not do that. Did not dare do that. No, she had already told him she did not want to marry him. He would not tread any further on the limb he occupied, lest it break and fall free from the tree entirely.

"What is the condition?" he asked carefully.

"That you accept mine as well." Her blue-green gaze studied him, seeing far more—he had no doubt—than he wanted her to see. "Will you, Gill? I am sorry for hurting you."

Hurt.

That lone word terrified him.

It took him back to the lad he had been. The helpless lad. Locked in the chamber. His father had hurt him again and again, until he had taught himself not to care. He had spent all the years since then doing his best not to give a damn about anyone other than his brother.

"I accept your apology," he rasped, growing even more uncomfortable.

"Good." She smiled, and damn him, there was her dimple, making another appearance. "I accept yours as well."

"Good." He cleared his throat again, reminded once more of the impropriety of their situation. Of the foolishness. "You should go before you are seen here. Before neither of us has a choice."

But instead of leaving, she cocked her head at him. "Why do you want to marry me, Gill?"

Bloody hell, what manner of question was that?

He struggled to form an answer, but the responses in his mind were none he could bear to say aloud.

Because I want to spend the rest of my life kissing you.

Because you make me laugh.

Because you are the only woman who has ever found a way past my defensive walls.

Hell. She had not just found a way around them. She had dismantled them like a barrage of cannon fire. Left them crumbling around him.

But he would not speak of any of those things.

"My estates are in ruin," he said. "My father squandered the family's vast fortune, and the coffers need replenishment. I need a bride with a generous dowry."

That, too, was the truth. But it was not the only truth.

She stiffened. "You wished to marry me for the Winter fortune?"

Damnation, what a cad he sounded like when she phrased it thus.

"That is not the sole motivation in wanting you as my duchess," he hastened to explain. "I also like you...admire you, even."

Somehow, his lips could not form around the word *love*.

His tongue could not even prepare the consonant.

Because love was dangerous. Love invited pain. He had loved his father, once. Before his father had broken him. Look at the husk of a man that remained.

"You like me," she repeated dully.

"A great deal," he added.

"And admire me."

He nodded, a sick sensation settling in his gut which told him he was not helping his cause. "Yes."

Her ordinarily lush lips tightened. "You want to marry me because you require my share of the Winter fortune, and because you like and admire me."

Bloody hell. The tone of her voice was surely a harbinger of doom.

He wanted to say more, but the familiar prickle of perspiration on his brow and the thudding of his heart warned him of a different sort of doom entirely.

The affliction.

"Yes," was all he could manage. Because somewhere deep inside him, he was locked inside that dark chamber.

His father had told him he was weak, and he was. Gill had proven it again and again. Though his bastard of a sire had perished, his legacy lived on.

"Then I stand firm in my decision," she told him. "I am glad to see you are not suffering from a lung infection as my sister supposed. Indeed, you seem quite hale for one who has been hiding within his chamber for the span of a day."

He had not been hiding. He had been waiting. Waiting for her to come to him.

But instead of winning her over, he had further pushed her away. He could read it in her eyes. See it in the stubborn set of her chin. In the grim clench of her jaw. Perhaps, this time he had pushed her too far. Further than he would be able to reach.

Perhaps it was just as well.

Perhaps there was, just as Father had always scornfully insisted, something inherently wrong with him. Christabella would do far better to find a whole man. One who could love her as she deserved. Not a man who was too bound by the past to allow himself to feel.

Yes, if he cared for her, there was only one answer. And he saw it now with a grim resolution. He had been wrong, terribly wrong, to think he could find happiness. That he deserved it. That he was worthy of someone as beautiful, sparkling, and wonderful as Miss Christabella Winter.

For he was most decidedly not.

"Marry another gentleman, Miss Winter," he said harshly, though the words broke him apart inside. "One who is more worthy than I could ever hope to be. Whoever he is, I wish you happy with him."

"Gill," she protested, her certainty seeming to crumble before his eyes.

He would have to be resolute.

"You may address me as Your Grace, Miss Winter," he told her in his frostiest ducal accents. The ones he scarcely ever had cause to use.

Mostly because his tongue ordinarily refused to function.

She recoiled, taking a step back as if he had struck her. "Of course. Forgive me my familiarity, Your Grace. I will go now and leave you to your illness. I, too, wish you happy."

With that grim, parting volley, she dipped into a hasty curtsy.

Before he could regret his words, she was gone.

And when the door slammed closed and he was alone once more, that was when the regret truly hit him. Hit him like the weight of a bloody stone castle wall falling upon him.

He knew, with devastating certainty, that he had just lost his only chance of ever finding happiness. If indeed he had ever had one to begin with.

CHRISTABELLA DID NOT want to marry someone else.

She wanted to marry Gill.

Infuriating, handsome, irritating, aloof, confusing, wonderful, frustrating Gill. The Duke of Coventry. The man she was going to marry. Even if he was wrong about everything he had just said to her. Even if she would as soon turn back to his chamber and rail at him as tell him she loved him.

Love, yes.

That was what she felt for him. Her sisters had not been wrong. Her heart beat for one man, and one man alone. Christabella knew it now, and the realization was one part welcoming acceptance, one part blistering confusion. For he had not spoken of love to her. He had used a different "L" word entirely.

Like.

How tepid. How irritating. Also, how wrong.

Because Gill was in love with her, just as she was in love with him. Both against their wills, perhaps. It had simply happened, however. Naturally. Instinctively. Beautifully.

Oh, yes. No question of it: she was going to marry that man.

She reached her decision sometime between her initial flight from his chamber—in humiliated tears—and her second crash into Lady Adele Saltisford somewhere in the vast maze of the eastern wing of Abingdon House.

One moment, she was hurrying down the corridor, her vision blurred, hot tracks of outrage and sadness burning down her cheeks, attempting to find a means by which she could make Gill see reason, and the next, she was rounding a bend and hurtling herself into poor Lady Adele.

This time, Lady Adele bore the brunt of their collision. She went flying to her rump whilst Christabella hovered over her, immobile. She had not fallen. Nor had she lost her balance or equilibrium. And strangely, the tears had stopped.

Because she had a path now. Even if it involved potentially boxing the Duke of Coventry's ears to make him see reason. He would see it. She would force him to. She had an untold arsenal, after all, filled with snowballs, tickling, laughter, and kisses. All of which he had already proven himself most susceptible to indeed.

He was going to make her victory appallingly easy.

But there was no time to dwell upon her impending triumph, for Lady Adele was still sprawled upon the floor.

Christabella lowered to her knees and grasped Lady Adele's hands in hers, leveraging her to a sitting position. "Have I caused you injury?" she asked, hating the thought of having hurt Lady Adele in some fashion, all because of her confused feelings and her haste.

"Forgive me, Miss Winter," Lady Adele said, seeming to collect herself after her initial stunned response. "I am once again in err, not watching where I am traveling, and moving with far too great a haste."

It did not escape her notice that Lady Adele was pale indeed.

"Are you feeling well, my lady?" she ventured.

Lady Adele's expression was pinched. Closed in upon itself. "Perfectly well, thank you, Miss Winter. I must insist you call me Adele. No formality between us, if you please."

"Then you shall call me Christabella," she countered, offering her unlikely new friend a hand. "May I help you to stand?"

She felt guilty for having repeatedly run into Lady Adele, who had only been gracious and lovely. And entirely forgiving of the sights she had witnessed—not to mention perhaps overheard—between Christabella and Gill, loyally remaining silent. Nary a hint of gossip had been spread.

Lady Adele took her hand, allowing Christabella to help her to her feet. They stood opposite each other in the hall, taking each other's measures.

"Christabella," Lady Adele said at length with a nod of her head, as if she had reached a conclusion.

"Adele," she returned, equally hesitant. "Are you certain nothing is amiss? You look frightfully pale, almost as if you are ill."

"And you look the same," said the other lady, quite shrewdly. "Unless I am mistaken, there are the trails of tears on your cheeks. Your nose is quite red. And I do believe you have come from the direction of the Duke of Coventry's chamber."

Here was a worthy opponent.

Lady Adele was sharp-witted. Kind, and yet she clearly possessed a calculating side. Christabella approved.

"We are all allowed our secrets, are we not?" she asked softly. "You have more than enough of your own, I would wager."

"I do, and speaking of them…" Lady Adele paused, then inclined her head. "I have been meaning to speak with you concerning the favor I asked."

Christabella could not help but to take note of her pallor once again. "Are you certain nothing is amiss?"

Lady Adele swallowed, looking as if she were ill. "Everything is amiss, I am afraid, and it is all my fault, but that matters not. What does matter is the favor. If you cannot do it, I understand. Please know that regardless of your decision, your secret is safe with me."

Her secret involving Gill.

The man she loved.

The man she had to find some way of convincing to marry her. The man she had to make realize he loved her every bit as much as she loved him. Stubborn virgin rakehell that he was.

"Thank you," she said simply, turning her attention back to the discussion at hand. "Please, do tell me what it is that you require. I will be happy to help however I may."

Lady Adele hesitated, as if she were struggling to find the proper words. "I was wondering if you might convince my older sister that you have invited me to remain here with your family as a guest, beyond Christmastide."

It was not the sort of favor Christabella would have guessed she would request. And certainly surprising, coming from a duke's daughter. Why would Lady Adele wish to remain?

"You want to stay on at Abingdon House?" she asked. "Consider it done. My brother is remaining in residence for at least the next fortnight, before returning to London."

"That is the crux of the matter, I am afraid, and the necessity for the favor," Lady Adele said, her expression strained. "You see, I...need to go away. I am not certain just where yet, as I have not had the proper time to formulate my plan, but before I can do anything, I must convince my sister to leave me behind. That way, I will be unencumbered and free to make the decisions I must."

"But why must you go away?" Christabella's curiosity could not be restrained. "And why lie to your sister? Surely she would understand."

"This is a matter most delicate," Lady Adele said, her voice so low it was almost a whisper. "I dare not involve anyone else."

She struggled to comprehend what matter would lead to Lady Adele's flight and could think of only one thing. And that one thing seemed decidedly unlikely for a reserved, shy wallflower.

"Will you not confide in me, at least?" she asked, feeling a strong surge of empathy for the other woman. "If you are in trouble, perhaps I may be of assistance."

"I am in trouble, but the trouble is of my own making." Lady Adele paused, biting her lip and pressing a hand over her abdomen. "I do not want anyone else to be hurt by what I have done, and that includes you, Miss Winter. You will grant me all the aid I require in persuading my sister to allow me to linger here."

"But where will you go, if you have no intention to remain here at Abingdon Hall?" she pressed. "You can hardly intend to disappear. A lady such as yourself, alone in the world...why, it would be dangerous."

"Not any more dangerous than the future facing me, I fear." Lady Adele looked grim.

Christabella could not help but to wonder how her future could be so grim when she was the daughter of a duke. When she was lovely, her lineage impeccable, her deportment forever above reproach.

But she said nothing, for her newfound friend seemed to wish to guard her secrets. "Whatever happens," she said, speaking as much to herself as to Lady Adele, "everything will work out as it ought. Even if it seems impossible."

She had to believe it, for without hope, what remained?

Chapter Eleven

"*Y*OU HAVE SURRENDERED," Ash pronounced, disgust evident in his tone. "By God, Gill, I never thought I would see the day."

Morning had dawned grim and bleak, just as the day before had been. But he and his brother were on their customary ride despite the threat of another snowfall looming on the horizon. It was rather indicative of Gill's mood.

He had spent the remainder of yesterday wallowing in his own self-pity to such a degree that he had actually called for some brandy. He had fallen into bed in a stupor and had risen to the devil's own headache.

Along with the unshakeable heartache that had been his steady companion since he had watched Christabella Winter walk out of his bedchamber—and mayhap his life—the day before.

"I did not surrender," he corrected his brother at length, his voice sharper than he intended as he defended himself. "I did the only thing I could do."

"The only thing to do is to wed her, and yet you told her to marry someone else."

His brother was irritatingly right.

He winced. The day was deuced cold, as was the rapidly dawning fear he had made an insurmountable mistake. "I did what was right, what was fair. Christabella deserves a man who can love her. I am incapable of it."

Ash scoffed. "What rot. You think yourself incapable of love?"

"There is something inherently wrong with me," he said, shifting uncomfortably in his saddle. "Whatever softness I had was beaten out of me by our father, or lost somewhere deep inside the chamber where he kept me locked for days on end."

"The bastard locked you in a chamber?" Ash demanded.

Belatedly, Gill realized how much he had just revealed.

More than he had wanted, it was true.

"Occasionally," he muttered. "It was nothing, and many years ago now. Do not worry yourself over it."

"It happened when I was sent to stay with Mother in London, was it not?" Ash asked, his jaw rigid.

"It did," he admitted.

Their father had made certain to separate them often in their youth. Though he had claimed it was because he wished his heir to follow in his shadow whilst a mere second son was extra trouble he did not need, Gill saw quite suddenly the reason why. When the brothers had been separated, they were unable to defend each other against their father's wrath.

Thus it had remained until, eventually, they had grown too tall and strong to suffer their father's abuse any longer. He had turned his perversity to his mistresses then, the despicable sort of man who took pleasure in the pain of others.

"Damn it to hell, Gill, why did you not tell me?" Ash demanded. "I would have done something to try to stop him. We could have banded together."

"That is why I did not tell you." He looked away, gazing into the trees in the distance ahead.

Bereft of their leaves, their wizened branches were raised to the sky like open hands. Waiting for something. Something that would never come.

"I should have killed him before the devil took him," Ash growled.

Gill glanced back to his brother. "And that is another reason why I never told you. You have found happiness now. You deserve it, Ash. Leave the past where it belongs."

"Tell yourself the same bloody thing," his brother said.

"I am...as happy as I am capable of being," he said, struggling to give voice to the complex emotions churning through him.

"Horse shit," Ash spat. "You want to marry the hellion, and yet instead of fighting for her, you are giving in, allowing an enemy army to storm your bloody castle."

His brother's words produced a visceral reaction in him that he could neither deny nor control. The notion of another man touching Christabella made him want to slam his first through something.

"I am not giving in," he denied again, though this time with considerably less vehemence.

"Damn right you are not." Ash's countenance was determined. Stubborn. "Because I am not going to allow you to do something so cursed foolhardy. You are every bit as capable of being happy as I am. You said it yourself, Gill. Leave the past where it belongs. Do not allow that miserable prick to rule the rest of your life and ruin it from the grave."

Was that what he was doing?

His brother's words gave him pause.

"But what if he was right? There is something wrong with me, Ash," he said. "You cannot deny it. I freeze in large gatherings. I can scarcely speak."

"There is nothing wrong with you except that you are being a stubborn, wrongheaded fool," his brother accused. "There is no other explanation for what you are doing. You love Miss Christabella, do you not?"

Did he?

His heart was pounding, his ears going hot despite the frigid late December's winds tearing at him. "How did you know you were in love with Miss Prudence?"

"I realized I could not fathom spending one day without her," Ash answered. "That her kindness and beauty are mesmerizing. That her kisses drive me mad. That I could not bear to be anything other than hers."

Bloody hell.

It sounded familiar.

He reined in his horse, drawing to a stop. What if everything Ash had said was right? And what if he was a fool who had given up with far too much ease?

What if he *loved* Miss Christabella Winter?

"I need to return to Abingdon House immediately," he said.

"Yes," his brother agreed. "You do."

Because he *did* love Miss Christabella Winter. She owned his heart. His heart was capable of feeling. He had just been too deuced stupid to see it. But he was going to change that now, if it was the last thing he did.

"Carry on without me," he told Ash, turning his mount around to head back in the direction they had just come from.

"Do not forget to grovel," called his brother after him.

But Gill was riding too hard back to Christabella to answer.

CHRISTABELLA WAS WAITING for Gill in his chamber. Making her way there had been no easy feat. Ever since Pru and Lord Ashley had been caught alone together in dishabille by one of the servants, Dev had extra staff prowling the halls.

Lady Emilia was keeping a watchful eye upon all the Winter sisters as well.

Dev had held a private family meeting late yesterday evening, and he had been stern.

No more improprieties. Not even with their betrotheds. There was to be no sneaking about, no meeting alone, no stolen kisses.

In short, nothing fun.

But when Christabella had suggested as much, her brother's expression had turned thunderous. Though she and her sisters had quietly snickered at her sally, Dev had unsmilingly gone into yet another lecture. Her lack of foresight had earned her the rather sharp elbow of her sister, Grace, in her side.

And so it was not without great risk or the very real danger of inciting her brother's wrath that she had found her way back to Gill's chamber this morning. She knew from Pru that he and Lord Ashley had a habit of riding each morning. She knew when he left, when to expect his return.

She was prepared. She had been pacing the floor, practicing her speech for the last half hour. Christabella was not going to leave without making him listen to her. She had decided she must fight for them, even if he would not.

By her estimate, she had another half hour to prepare herself before—

The door to his chamber flew open, and he strode over the threshold, his high cheekbones still painted red from the chill outside. He was so caught up in his own thoughts he did not even see her at first. He came striding in, throwing the door closed behind him.

It was now, she told herself, or never.

"Gill," she said.

He jolted, as if jarred from slumber, his gaze flying to where she stood. "Christabella?"

"I need to speak with you," they both said in unison.

Then they stared at each other for a heavy, silent beat.

"Before you say anything, please listen," she began, only to stop when she realized they were once again speaking at the same time.

"I want to apologize," he was also saying, before pausing.

She longed to run to him. To end this silly distance between them. To throw her arms around him and feel his embrace surrounding her, inhale his familiar scent, absorb the steady beat of his heart.

"I want to apologize to you as well," she told him, remaining where she was, too uncertain of herself to move for the moment. "I am sorry, Gill, for not accepting your proposal of marriage when I had the chance. I was wrong."

"You were not wrong to refuse me," he countered, surprising her then by moving forward of his own volition. "I am no Lothario, as you well know. But I wish to God I had tried harder to tell you how much you mean to me. How much you have changed every part of me."

She took his hands in hers. They were cool from his time spent in the elements, but thankfully bare and devoid of gloves. She laced her fingers through his just the same. "I do not want or need a Lothario. All I want, and all I need, and all I love is you."

The confession left her feeling freer. Lighter. Also frightened.

Gill was staring at her, wordless.

Perhaps she had frightened him away. Perhaps whatever it was that rendered it so difficult for him to speak in social gatherings had returned.

Or perhaps he did not love her.

After all, he had only told her previously that he liked her.

She vowed not to let that sway her from her course. "I

came here to tell you that I do not want to marry anyone else. You are the only man for me. The only man I wish to wed. It must be you, or no one else. Unless you will not have me, of course. If you have changed your mind, I understand..."

"Of course I have not," he said in a rush, his fingers tightening on hers. "I have realized how wrong I was. Because the thought of you marrying anyone other than me is... Belle, I-I—"

He extended the sound of the I, seeming to struggle within himself.

She was about to tell him it did not matter, that she loved him enough, and that in time, she hoped his feelings for her would grow, when he shocked her.

"I love you," he blurted, so quickly she may have missed it had she not been hanging upon his every breath, his every word.

Gill's expression was pained. His jaw rigid. He was holding her hands in the tightest grip, as if he feared an incremental loosening of his hold on her would somehow make her disappear.

And all she could think was *thank merciful heavens.*

"I love you too," she said, beaming at him, unable to contain her happiness. "I love you so much it hurts. I am sorry it took me some time to puzzle out my emotions, and I am sorry that I allowed my pride to get in the way. When I thought you only wanted the Winter fortune instead of me, it hurt. I reacted foolishly. Selfishly. But when I thought about everything I know about you, about the way I feel for you, I knew I was wrong."

"You were not wrong." He shook his head. "You were right. I do not blame you one whit. I was the arse. Can you forgive me?"

"Of course." She bit her lip, searching his gaze. "You were

not the arse at all, Gill, You were…"

"The arse," he said again, offering her a wry grin that somehow only made him more handsome. More beloved.

"Do you still wish to marry me?" she asked, knowing she was taking a risk and doing so anyway.

"Bloody hell, woman, do you need to ask?" He lowered his head, pressing his forehead to hers, their entwined fingers trapped between their bodies. "There is nothing I want more than you at my side for the rest of my life, as my duchess. Not because of the blasted Winter fortune. But because of you, Belle. I love you. You changed me. Cut the bonds of my past and set me free."

His past.

It was the first time he had mentioned it.

But she had wondered, many times, what could have happened to him. What had turned him into the man he had become.

"I love you too, my darling man," she told him, releasing his hands to frame his beloved face. The prickle of his golden whiskers on her skin was a beautiful abrasion. She could not help but to wonder how it would feel rasping on her breasts. Or lower still…

"About my past, Belle," he began hesitantly, seeming to struggle in his search for the words.

Just like that, Christabella felt as if she were back to the day their paths had crossed in the salon. That first day. She had spoken for him. And he had not minded. Rather, her daring had entertained him, if vexed him.

"Your past is what makes you the man you are today," she told him then. "And the man you are is the man I fell in love with. That is all I need to know."

His eyes slid closed. "My father told me I was worthless. He was disappointed in me. I was the heir, and yet, I could not conduct myself as he expected I should. I was shy and quiet as a lad. He told me he would make me stronger by one means or another. And he tried. With a crop, with his fists. Sometimes, he would lock me in a windowless chamber for days. My mother, God save her soul, did not care what he did with me. She was far too busy with her own lovers. Lord knows what happened to Ash whilst he was in her care..."

Tears welled in her eyes. Pain sliced through her for the young man he must have been, for the pain and suffering he had endured at the hands of his own father. Her father, too, had been cruel. But he had been mostly absent. Any violence he had attempted to visit upon them had been swiftly canceled by Dev, who was old enough and large enough to be their protector.

But Gill was the eldest.

He had borne the brunt of his father's cruelty.

And *oh*, how her heart ached for him.

"My darling," she said, pressing her lips to his for a chaste kiss that was branded by the salty wetness of her own tears. "I am so very sorry."

His eyes opened, searing into hers. "I am not sorry. He did not change me, you see. I am as I have always been. Crowded ballrooms make me want to retch into the nearest potted palm, and I suspect they always will. Speaking in front of a gathering makes my heart pound and my skin feel as if it is too tight for my body. I am abysmal as a duke. I have so many people relying upon me, and yet I am most comfortable laboring amongst my tenants. Physical duty puts me at ease. As do you."

She was glad she put him at ease. Her thumbs swept over the proud architecture of his cheekbones. "I am so pleased I put you at ease, my darling. And I promise now and forevermore that as your duchess, if you want to retch into a potted palm, I shall stand before you and obstruct you from view. If you need to speak in front of a gathering, I will gladly do it for you. I also know you are a good duke, a wise duke, a fair duke. I know that because I know *you*, and I would be proud to be your wife and stand at your side."

He exhaled slowly. "I do not know what I did to become so fortunate."

"Nor do I," she returned, smiling into his eyes. "But I will gladly accept all the spoils of my fortune, so long as it involves becoming your duchess."

"I love you," he said, reverence making his voice tremble.

"And I love you," she said again, for it did not matter how many times she spoke the words aloud.

Indeed, it almost seemed the more times, the better.

"I am going to ask you a third time, Belle. This time, I am going to bloody well do it right." He paused, lifting their linked hands to his lips so he could place reverent kisses upon the tops of her hands. "Christabella Winter, you have filled my life with a light I did not even know existed. From the moment you entered the salon that day, you changed everything. I have never met a more maddening, fascinating, vexing, beautiful woman."

"Maddening?" she could not help but to protest with a teasing smile. "Vexing?"

"You tickled me," he pointed out. "And then you smelled me."

Well, yes, when he phrased it thus…

"You also pelted me with snowballs," he added.

She bit her lip to stifle her laughter. "You hit my bonnet with one."

"You taught me how to kiss," he continued, his gaze burning into hers.

"I rather thought you taught me," she said as wicked heat

flared to life in her core.

"You also taught me how to love." He kissed her hands again, then drew her more solidly against his body. "I love you, Christabella. Will you do me the great honor of marrying me?"

"Oh, Gill." Her heart beat so hard, so fast, it threatened to fly from her chest and soar among the clouds. Happiness and love washed over her, so profound, so humbling. "I would be honored to be your wife."

"Truly?" he asked.

"Truly," she said.

"Good. Because I am reasonably certain I will perish if I go another minute without kissing you."

His mouth was on hers in the next breath. Christabella looped her arms around his neck and rose on her toes, kissing him back with all the love and happiness blossoming to life within her.

Chapter Twelve

Three weeks later

*H*ER HUSBAND'S HAND was on her thigh.
Husband.

One word, two syllables. Such a tepid way to describe the man who had become everything to her.

She cast a sidelong glance at Gill's handsome profile. It was difficult to believe he was finally *hers*. It seemed they had waited forever for the banns to be read. But at long last, earlier that morning in the Abingdon Hall chapel, they had been married. Now, they were surrounded by family and a handful of friends who had remained, enjoying the wedding cake in the wake of the immense breakfast spread which had been served.

"I love you," Gill whispered in her ear, his lips near enough to graze her skin and send a shiver trilling down her spine.

The cake was delicious, but not nearly as delicious as her husband was.

Not to mention the prospect of consummating their union.

Beneath her beautiful gown and calm façade, she was positively aflame. Over the course of the last few weeks, they had found time to be alone together as Gill had stayed on at Abingdon Hall after the house party's conclusion. But though they had enjoyed some quiet moments of passion, they had yet to make love.

The wait was almost over.

She settled her hand in her lap, fingers resting over his, and gave him a gentle squeeze before slowly guiding his hand higher. It was wicked of her, she knew, for they were surrounded by others. But she could not help herself.

She stopped when his hand rested over the place where she ached for him the most.

"I love you too," she murmured back to him.

"Do stop whispering," Grace said. "It is insufferably rude."

Christabella laughed. "You are merely frustrated because your wedding has been delayed to accommodate for the arrival of the dowager Duchess of Revelstoke."

Grace and her betrothed, Viscount Aylesford, were wedding in another week to allow his grandmother time enough to arrive from Scotland. Grace's patience had grown thin. It was plain to see her sister was ready to become a wife.

"Who would have thought," Pru said, smiling at Lord Ashley, whom she had already married three days prior. "All the Winters found happiness and love in the span of a year."

Suddenly, a commotion could be heard in the great hall. Raised voices preceded the frantic scrambling of footsteps. Christabella stiffened, clutching her husband's arm in an instinctive gesture, for she could not fathom any event which would cause such a reaction save a fire. Oh, how she hoped Abingdon House would not burn to a heaping pile of ancestral rubble. She had grown rather fond of the massive old edifice.

Dev had already sprung to his feet when the door to the room burst open.

A tall, dark-haired man swept into the chamber, still clad

in his travel clothes, carrying a walking stick. There was something strangely familiar about him, although she was certain she had never before seen him. Lady Adele, seated quite near to Christabella at the table, let out a gasp.

Behind the man arrived a gaggle of servants, including a winded butler who apologized profusely to the gathering before turning his attention to the intruder.

"Sir, I am going to have to ask you to leave," he told the man pointedly.

The man simply raised his walking stick and withdrew the hollow end of it to reveal a sword. All this, he performed with a dangerous *ennui* that sent a chill down Christabella's spine.

"I've already silenced one of you with my fists," he drawled to the butler, his voice cold and hard. "If I am forced to silence another, I'll not be responsible for the bloodshed."

Gill stood up suddenly at her side, as did all the other gentlemen in attendance—Mr. Hart, Lord Hertford, Lord Aylesford, and Lord Ashley.

"What the devil are you doing here?" Dev demanded, his voice carrying the sting of a whip's lash.

"Forgive me," said the interloper, scorn dripping from his voice. "It looks as if I have interrupted a wedding breakfast. My invitation must have been lost."

Dev looked as if he wanted to do murder. He gripped the back of his chair, scowling. "You are not welcome on my lands," he growled, his tone laden with fury and menace.

"Your lands?" the stranger mocked. "Ah, yes, you bought it just as you buy everything and everyone."

The enmity between her brother and the menacing man was palpable.

"Why the hell are you here?" Dev asked.

"I have come for what is mine," the man said, his gaze hovering on Lady Adele before flicking to Dev. "At long last."

Lady Adele was ashen, fear evident on her lovely face.

"Nothing here is yours," Dev warned.

"I suppose blood means nothing to you," the stranger said coldly.

Blood? Christabella stared hard at the man, then turned her gaze to Dev. The similarities were remarkable. Both tall, broad, dark-haired. Their noses were the same...

"Go back to the rookeries where you belong," Dev snapped. "I will not allow you to hurt this family any more than you already have."

"I have no intention of hurting anyone as long as I get what I have come here for," sneered the man. "Fear not. The bastard Winters want no part of any of you. Attempt to become an aristocrat all you like. We earn our coin as we see fit and answer to no one, least of all Devereaux Winter."

Dear God.

The bastard Winters?

Could it be that this dangerous-looking stranger who had interrupted the wedding breakfast was...her half brother?

"We need to speak," Dev said grimly. "In private."

Christabella watched in shock as her brother and the stranger strode from the chamber. She could not help but to note, along with a sinking feeling of dread, that even their gait was the same. Stunned silence filled the chamber in the wake of their exit. The servants seemed to disappear.

"Who the devil is he?" asked Mr. Hart, looking as bewildered as Christabella felt.

"He is Dominic Winter," said Lady Adele, her expression stricken, "and I fear he has come here for me."

Epilogue

Three days later

$\mathcal{G}$ ILL DID NOT even say a word before he drew Christabella to him and kissed her. She kissed him back with all the sweet ardor he had come to expect from her, her arms around his neck. His tongue was in her mouth, and his hands went to her waist, anchoring her to him as he ravished her lips.

He was starving for her.

And at last, the long wait was over.

She was his wife. His duchess. His heart.

Now, he was going to make love to her for the first time.

Christabella had been the most beautiful bride he had ever beheld three days ago when they had wedded in the Abingdon Hall chapel. But she was even more beautiful tonight, at his country seat, in the duchess' apartments. Precisely where she belonged.

She had donned a dressing gown belted at the waist, covering her lush form in prim fashion. He wore a silk banyan, and each movement of it over his bare flesh had been an unfair tease of what was to come. It had been a caress, but not the one he wanted, not the one that had kept him longing all through the relentless days of wintry travel they had just endured. He had been determined not to take her for the first time in a carriage or an inn, and the additional wait, atop the three weeks for the banns to be read, meant that his cockstand was harder than a block of marble.

Despite the frigid weather, they had departed for their new home following the madness of the wedding breakfast. Dominic Winter's interruption had been unexpected. Shocking as hell for all parties, particularly the Winter sisters who had previously had no notion they possessed six illegitimate half-siblings.

Christabella broke the kiss and tipped back her head, her gaze searching his. "Do you think we did the right thing, Gill?"

Bloody hell, doubt was not what he wanted to hear at this particular juncture.

He raised a hand to cup her silken cheek. "Marrying each other?"

A tender smile curved her kiss-swollen lips. "No. Of course not marrying, my love. No decision was ever better. I meant in leaving Abingdon Hall behind with so much unsettled."

Ah, of course.

She had been worrying over their departure since the moment their carriage had rolled down the tree-lined drive as previously planned. He could not blame her, for Dominic Winter was not the sort of man to inspire feelings of comfort. From the moment he had stalked into the wedding breakfast, bearing his walking stick with the hidden blade, sneering as if he found them all contemptible, Gill had known the man was trouble.

"I know we did the right thing, Belle," he comforted her. "Your brother has Ash, Hertford, Hart, and Aylesford there with him. And Mr. Winter can only wreak so much havoc."

"I can still scarcely believe I have six siblings, that my father had a whole family I had no inkling existed." A frown furrowed her brow. "But how could Dev know and keep it from us?"

"It is as your brother said," he reassured. "He was not convinced the claims were legitimate. He was only seeking to protect you."

He refrained from pointing out the obvious, which was that if it became common knowledge the Wicked Winters shared blood with a family who ruled the London underworld, not even the vast Winter fortune would have induced most noble families to take on such a mésalliance.

Gill was not bothered by the connection, for he was in love with Christabella herself and not the coin she would bring to their union. No scandal, and no tie to London's rookeries could keep him from making her his. However, he could well understand the overly protective Devereaux Winter seeking to shield his sisters from further gossip. Even if it meant keeping the secret to himself.

However, the secret had now been revealed.

"He should have told us," Christabella insisted. "We all had a right to know."

"Knowing you as I do, I expect he feared you would attempt to flee to the rookeries to meet these supposed siblings," he told his wife, stroking his thumb over her cheekbone. "What would you have done if a pickpocket or other cutthroat had descended upon you and done you harm? Tickling would not have worked in such a scenario."

Indeed, the very notion of his vibrant, bold wife sneaking to London's worst stews made a shiver roll down his spine.

"I would never have gone to the rookeries," she denied stubbornly. "But I deserved to know about Mr. Winter and his siblings. *My* siblings."

"You would have gone there," he countered gently, knowingly. "We both know it, Belle. However, I do agree with you that your brother should have at least made you aware of the existence of the other Winters. Some secrets are better shared than kept."

"Yes," she agreed. "Oh, Gill, this is why I love you so. You always know how to cut to the heart of a matter."

Sometimes in the wrong fashion entirely, but he refrained from offering that aloud.

Instead, he decided to tease her. "It is not the only reason, I hope."

"Of course it is not." Her smile deepened, and there was the dimple that haunted him in his sleep. "I love you for many other reasons as well. Because you are kind, softhearted, and good. Because you laugh at my sallies. Also because you are a wondrous kisser. Because I cannot resist you…hmm…and because you love me too, and because you are going to take me to visit my new siblings when we return to London…"

He frowned. "I appreciate all of those reasons. Save the last. We do not even know if these potential siblings of yours are trustworthy. The man had a blade hidden in his walking stick, for heaven's sake."

"He is well-prepared," she argued in true Christabella Winter fashion.

Strike that.

In true Christabella *Coventry* fashion.

And that was one of the many reasons why *he* loved *her*.

She had an indefatigable ability to see the best in everyone. Including him. And damn it, if she wanted to meet these other Winters, these Winters who were most certainly even more wicked than the Wicked Winters could ever hope to be, she would meet them, *by God*. And he would accompany her. But first, he had to see about commissioning a walking stick that contained a hidden sword…

"If it is your wish to become acquainted with Mr. Winter and his siblings, it will be done," he told her.

"Truly?" she asked, her smile deepening.

"Truly," he vowed, and then could not resist kissing that dimple of hers. "Whatever Her Grace wishes, Her Grace gets. By the rules of the house."

Her smile turned naughty then. "I like the rules of the house. Because right now, what I want more than anything is my husband."

Just like that, his cock was rigid and ready once more.

"Then your husband you shall have, my darling." He kissed her.

She opened for him, her tongue meeting his. Her fingers sank into his hair as she pulled him even closer. He inhaled deeply of her scent. Blossoms and summer sun and everything bold and bright and wonderful. Everything that was filled with hope.

He inhaled that hope, and he kissed her with everything he had. They had been practicing, after all. The nights had been long, staying on those bloody uncomfortable inn beds, not making love to his wife as he longed. But he had been determined. Stubborn, it was true. He wanted their first time—both of their first times—to be perfect.

He wanted to begin their life together where they would live it out, and where he felt most comfortable—at his country seat. This was a place of hard work and joy. It was just the place for a new start.

They moved as one, kissing, crossing the chamber, moving slowly toward the bed. His fingers found the knot of her dressing gown, plucking it open. The ends of her robe gaped, and he slid it from her shoulders. The night rail she wore beneath was thin and soft, so bloody soft. But not as soft as her skin. He absorbed her heat, her curves. Every inch of her he could.

He was so lost in her, in fact, that he walked them right

into the bed without realizing it. They lost their balance and fell, together, upon it. He used his arms to leverage himself, attempting not to crush her. Their lips parted. Mutual laughter bubbled up, ringing forth.

Damn, but he loved her laugh.

He loved *her*, and it was at least the thousandth time he had entertained just such a sentiment in the last few weeks, but it was every bit as true.

"My seduction of you is decidedly not going according to plan," he admitted, falling into her green-blue eyes the same way he had fallen into the bed. "I feel like an oaf."

Her tender smile pierced his heart. "You do not resemble an oaf in the slightest, my darling husband."

"Did I injure you?" he asked, searching her face.

He felt certain he had borne the brunt of their impact. She did not appear winded.

She giggled again. "No. Now do stop fretting and make love to me."

A more promising invitation had never been issued, he was sure. His cock twitched to life once more as he realized he was settled nicely between her thighs. Just where he longed to be. He was not a practiced rake like his brother, but he was fairly confident he could follow his instincts and bring both of them great pleasure. The time leading up to and following their nuptials had not precisely been chaste, even if they had not consummated their relationship.

"As you command, Your Grace," he told her, and then he could not resist dipping his head to kiss her sweet lips once more.

She kissed him back, their tongues mating. He could kiss her like this forever, he thought. But there were other, equally delicious places to press his mouth upon her body. To taste her. He kissed down her throat and then peeled his body away from hers long enough to whip her night rail over her head.

She was bared to his worshiping gaze. He wanted to drink her in, but he also wanted to consume her. It was a hell of a conundrum. Her breasts were perfect, round swells. He cupped one in his palm and lowered his head, sucking the hard, pink peak into his mouth.

Her soft cry and the instant arch of her back told him she liked it.

So he did it again. Then he fluttered his tongue over her, licking her. Learning her. The taut bud puckered. He moved to her other breast, kissing the generous fullness before sucking her nipple into his mouth.

"Oh, Gill."

His name on her lips, in her husky voice, was the greatest reward. And all he could think of was kissing her everywhere. Licking her everywhere. Until she was writhing and helpless beneath him. He traveled farther, kissing down her creamy skin, tasting her. Her skin was sweet, salty, and she smelled faintly of flowers. But he wanted more.

He slid away from her, lowering to his knees on the carpet. Her legs were spread, opening her to him. Her cunny was there, and though he had touched that paradise on past occasions, this was his first glimpse. It was better than any engraving or painting he had ever seen. Better than his imagination.

Her cunny was pink, glistening, like the petals of the rarest flower. Her mound was shielded by a womanly thatch of cinnamon curls. Need roared through him, rendering him immobile until the scent of her reached him. Musky and delicious. He had to taste.

His hands swept up her inner thighs, opening her more, and she moved with him, complicit. Wanting. Watching. Waiting.

"You are the most beautiful sight I have ever beheld," he told her honestly, his voice quivering with emotion.

She moaned, moving her bottom on the bed as if in invitation.

And he did not hesitate. He lowered his head, licking her slit. She was wet, and she tasted even sweeter here, at the heart of her. He licked into her channel, finding it with ease. She rocked her hips, thrusting against his face. He slid his hands up her thighs, over her hips, until he was cupping her deliciously rounded bottom.

Perfection.

He held her to him, as if she were a feast.

In a sense, she was. Because he was starving. And though he had promised himself he would proceed slowly, he could not seem to regain his control. Desire for her slammed into him. He was a man consumed, sinking his tongue deeper before traveling higher, to the fleshy bud he had spied hidden within her folds.

Her pearl.

He sucked. Hard.

She cried out, bucking against him. Her fingers were in his hair, raking his scalp, tugging on the ends. She had turned into a wild woman in her frenzy. And he loved it. Because he felt the same way. All the advice his brother had given him, all the bawdy books he had read in an attempt to leave his wife well-pleased escaped him.

He was a man possessed now, following his instinct. Listening to Christabella's breathy sighs. Learning the urgency in her undulations. When she made intoxicating sounds low in her throat, and her hips moved seemingly of their own volition, he knew he had found a particularly sensitive place. He sucked, licked, used his teeth.

Suddenly, she stiffened beneath him, gasping his name.

He had made her spend, and the realization only served to heighten his own need. He flicked his tongue over her until the last ripples of her pleasure seemed to abate. And then he was on the bed with her, his body ready.

Her hands found the knot keeping his banyan in place.

He had forgotten, in the intensity of his need, that he was still clothed. As one, they removed the last impediment to their bodies being together. But she surprised him by urging him onto his back after he had shed the garment.

"Belle," he said, wondering what she was doing. Because he had to be inside her. Now.

"There is something I read about in a wicked book I managed to acquire," she told him, as if sensing the question in his mind. Her touch was on his chest now, caressing, leaving molten heat in its wake. Everywhere her fingers grazed, he felt alive. Alive and starving.

"You are beautiful too, Gill," she told him. "So strong. I love your chest."

She caressed him, then raked her nails over his flat nipples, which proved surprisingly sensitive. Lowering her head, she began kissing a path over his body in the same way he had done to her. The breath hissed from his lungs, the heat and hunger shooting to his already-rigid cock.

What the devil was she doing?

What had she read about?

He forgot to care—hell, he forgot the English language altogether—when she placed a kiss on his straining shaft. And when she took him into her mouth...

"Fuck," he moaned, the curse fleeing him. He could not control it. Could not contain it.

She was...

He was...

Bloody hell, those lips. His hips jerked, driving his cock

into her mouth. And she took him, making a soft whimper of her own pleasure. He was surrounded by wet heat. Her hum vibrated down his aching shaft, making his ballocks tighten.

He was going to spill.

If he did not stop her, he would not be able to hold back. And there was only one place he wanted to plant his seed this night. It was deep inside his wife.

Gently, he disengaged from her, before positioning them so that she was on her back and he atop her once more.

"I was just beginning," she protested.

He groaned, pressing his forehead to hers. "That is what I was afraid of, my darling. I cannot bear another moment of such torture. I need to be inside you."

"I want to try it again," she murmured. "I love your cock, Gill. It is so beautiful. It does seem frightfully large, however. How will it...fit, do you suppose? Inside me, that is?"

He suppressed another moan, because the mere thought of his cock inside her was enough to make him dangerously close to the edge. And because only Christabella would say such a thing. What else could he expect from the bold lady who had dared to tickle him, who had lured him from his shell?

Nothing less, and he knew it.

He kissed her, reaching between their bodies to find her cunny once more. She was dripping, so wet. That was important, and he knew it. With his forefinger, he found her pearl once more, stimulating her there until her hips were moving and her breath emerged in shallow gasps.

Until he could not wait.

He withdrew from her and used her dew, slicking it over his shaft.

He paused, tearing his mouth from hers. "Are you ready, my love?"

"Always," she said.

He guided his cock to her entrance. One pump of his hips, and he was seated inside her. Not all the way. Just enough. The sensation was exquisite. Unlike anything he could have fathomed. Tight heat engulfed him. He almost came right then.

But he held himself still, for he knew the loss of a woman's maidenhead could prove painful. He kissed her cheek, her nose. "How do you feel, Belle?"

"Incredible," she whispered back. "Why did you stop?"

"Is there pain?" he asked, mindful of her.

"A sting," she said, "nothing more. The greatest ache inside me only has one solution."

Bloody hell.

He moved again. Remembering the importance of her pearl, he worked it once more with his fingers, which had remained between their bodies. She was swollen, ready. She bowed from the bed, and he drove deeper. Then deeper. Until he was seated all the way, inside her as far as he could go.

Their mouths met.

They kissed, and it was fervent and carnal, those kisses. He could not keep still. His body had a mind of its own, his desire all-encompassing. Gill lost control. He withdrew from her almost entirely and then thrust home once more. The friction and tightness were making him mindless.

He and Christabella found a rhythm, moving together. It seemed as natural and right as anything. As natural and right as the two of them, as their love. Nothing had ever been so pure, so true. Their bodies and their hearts were one.

He increased his pressure on the bud of her sex, and she tightened on him, her sheath gripping him with so much force, he lost himself. Her spend rippled through her as he buried himself to the hilt. And it was too much. He tensed and spilled deep inside her. They came together, their cries mingling in the night.

The force of his release rolled through him, and he remained where he was, still inside her, spent. And sated. Oh, so damned sated.

Gill held his weight on his forearms, conscious enough not to want to smother her entirely beneath his much larger body. He kissed her once more, his gaze locking with hers.

"I love you, my darling Belle," he said.

He wanted to say more, but his mind was addled. He was mindless. Breathless. Helpless.

And happy.

So deliriously happy.

"I love you too," she told him, her caresses sweeping up and down the plane of his back. "When can we do that again?"

Gill did the only thing he could do in a moment like that.

He tipped back his head and laughed.

"Soon," he replied, pressing another kiss to her lips.

"Do you promise?" she murmured against his mouth, the minx he had married.

"I swear," he vowed.

"What about now?" she asked wickedly, moving her hips against his.

What about now, indeed? He kissed his wild Winter again.

And then again.

It proved a long, long time before either of them fell asleep that night, replete and happy and in love, wrapped in each other's arms.

THE END.

Dear Reader,

Thank you for reading *Wild in Winter*! I hope you enjoyed this sixth book in my The Wicked Winters series and that Gill and Christabella's unique love story touched your heart. I love my Winter family, and I thank you, the readers, for loving them too!

In fact, I love them so much that I'm not ready to say goodbye to them yet, and I hope you aren't either. The secret's out! The other half of the Winter family, led by oldest brother Dominic Winter, is about to start falling in love. Look for this continuation of the series in Fall 2020. I can't wait for you to meet the Wickedest Winters yet...

For more information on this and my other series, sign up for my newsletter (scarlettscottauthor.com/contact) or follow me on Amazon or BookBub. Join my reader's group on Facebook for bonus content, early excerpts, giveaways, and more.

As always, please consider leaving an honest review of *Wild in Winter*. Reviews are greatly appreciated!

While you wait for the next chapter of The Wicked Winters, why not check out my League of Dukes series if you haven't already? If you'd like a preview of *Scandalous Duke*, a steamy stand-alone romance about a single father duke on a dangerous mission and an American actress with secrets, do read on! It's got all the heart and sizzle of The Wicked Winters, but with an added dose of adventure.

Until next time,

Scarlett

Scandalous Duke

BY
SCARLETT SCOTT

Felix Markham, Duke of Winchelsea, has devoted his life to being the perfect statesman and raising his daughter after his beloved wife's death. But when devastating bombings on the railway leave London in an uproar, he is determined to bring the mastermind of the attacks to justice. He will lure the fox from his den by any means.

In her youth, Johanna McKenna donned a French accent and stage name to escape the clutches of her violent father and became the darling of the New York City stage as Rose Beaumont. Her past comes calling when her brother's reappearance in her life leads her into a dangerous web of deceit. She finds herself hopelessly trapped until she receives an offer she cannot refuse from London's most famous theater.

Felix's plan is clear: bring the famed Rose of New York to London, secure her as his mistress, and drive his quarry to English shores. But the more time he spends in Johanna's company, the more he realizes nothing is as it seems, least of all the woman who feels as if she were made to be in his arms. When he finally learns the truth, it may be too late to save both his city and the enigmatic lady who has stolen his heart.

Chapter One

London, 1883

FROM THE MOMENT he first saw Rose Beaumont grace the stage that evening, Felix had known why she was the most celebrated actress in New York City. He also knew why Drummond McKenna, the Fenian mastermind behind the explosions on the London railway, would want her in his bed. And he knew he was going to do his damnedest to use the beauty to lure McKenna to the justice awaiting him.

But for now, he would settle for champagne.

He took a sip, watching his quarry from across Theo Saville's sumptuous ballroom where the company of *The Tempest* and the city's most elite patrons of the arts had gathered to fête the Rose of New York. Trust Theo to throw a party lavish enough for an emperor. The servants were aplenty, the food was French, the champagne likely cost a small fortune, and the company was elegantly dissolute.

As a duke from a line that descended practically to the days of William the Conqueror, wealth and ostentation did not impress Felix. As a man who had lost the only woman he had ever loved, women did not ordinarily impress him either.

Rose Beaumont, however, did.

In the light of the gas lamps, she was a sight to behold. Dressed in an evening gown of rich claret, her golden hair worked into an elaborate Grecian braid, there was no doubt she commanded the eye of every gentleman in the chamber. Rubies and gold glinted from her creamy throat, her lush bosom and cinched waist on full display.

And though he observed her to hone his strategy, he could not deny he was as helplessly in awe of her as the rest of the sorry chaps gaping at her beauty. He had watched her perform, so mesmerized by her portrayal of Miranda, he had forgotten he was attending the theater to further his goal. For a brief beat, he forgot it anew as she tilted her head toward Theo and laughed at something droll he had no doubt said.

Theo looked pleased, and well he should, for though he had brought Rose Beaumont to his stage as a favor to Felix, there had been so much fanfare surrounding the arrival of the famed Rose of New York, that his already much-lauded theater was enjoying an unprecedented amount of attention. But he was also favoring Mademoiselle Beaumont with his rascal's grin, the one Felix had seen lead many a woman straight to his bed.

Felix had not painstakingly crafted his plan just so Theo could ruin it with his insatiable desire to get beneath a lady's skirts. No, indeed. Felix finished his champagne, deposited his empty glass upon a servant's tray, and then closed the distance between himself and his prey.

As he reached them, he realized, much to his irritation, that Rose Beaumont was lovelier than she had been from afar. Her eyes were a startling shade of blue, so cool, they verged on gray. Her lips were a full, pink pout. Her nose was charmingly retroussé. Hers was an ideal beauty, juxtaposed with the lush potency of a female who knew her power over the opposite sex.

Their gazes clashed, and he felt something deep inside him, an answering awareness he had not expected, like a jolt of sheer electricity to his senses. There was something visceral and potent in that exchange of glances. A current blazed down his spine, and his cock twitched to life.

She smelled of rose petals. Rose had been the scent Hattie favored. The realization and recognition made an unwanted stirring of memory wash over him. He banished the remembrance, for he could not bear to think of Hattie when he stood opposite a woman who had shared the bed of a monster like Drummond McKenna.

"Winchelsea," Theo greeted him warmly. "May I present to you Miss Rose Beaumont, lately of New York, the newest and loveliest addition to the Crown and Thorn?"

Her stare was still upon him. He looked at her and tried to feel revolted. But the disgust he had summoned for her when she had been nothing more than a name on paper refused to return. Her beauty was blinding, and he told himself that was the reason for his sudden, unaccountable vulnerability. That and the scent of her. Not just rose, he discovered, but an undercurrent of citrus. Distinctly different from Hattie's scent after all.

He offered a courtly bow. Though he no longer chased women, he recalled all too well how to woo, and he reminded himself now that this was a duty. One in a line of many he had spent in all his years as a devoted servant of Her Majesty.

"Mademoiselle Beaumont," he said when he straightened to his full height. "My most sincere compliments on your performance tonight. You were brilliant."

"Thank you," she said, her gaze inscrutable as it flitted over his face. "You are too kind."

Her husky voice reached inside him, formed a knot of desire he did not want to feel. Why did she have to be so damn beautiful? He cast a meaningful glance toward Theo, who had been his friend for many years. And who knew what was required of him in this instance.

"If you will excuse me," Theo said smoothly, "I must check in with my chef. The fellow is French and quite temperamental. Mademoiselle Beaumont, Winchelsea."

Theo departed with the sleek grace of a panther, leaving Felix alone with Mademoiselle Beaumont. His friend's defection occurred so abruptly, Felix found himself unprepared.

"That was badly done of him," Mademoiselle Beaumont said in the same voice that had brought the audience to their knees earlier that evening. It bore the trace of a French accent, one which had been notably absent from her earlier performance.

"I beg your pardon, Mademoiselle Beaumont?" he asked, perhaps in a sharper tone than he had intended.

He was out of his depths, and he knew it. He had procured mistresses before. He had been a statesman for all his life. He had been involved in complex investigations, harrowing danger, the aftermath of brutal violence. He had witnessed, firsthand, the wreckage of the rail carriages in the wake of the bombs, which had recently exploded.

But he had never attempted to make a Fenian's mistress *his* mistress.

"Mr. Saville," Mademoiselle Beaumont elaborated. "He was giving you the opportunity to speak with me, was he not?"

"I cannot say I am capable of speaking for Mr. Saville's motivations," he evaded.

The statement was a blatant prevarication, for Felix did know precisely what spurred his friend in every occasion: money and cunny with a love of the arts thrown in for good measure.

"Forgive me, but I have already forgotten your name," she said. "Was it Wintersby?"

"Winchelsea," he gritted, though she did not fool him.

He had seen the light of feminine interest in her gaze. She felt the attraction between them—base animal lust though it may be—as surely as he did. Some time may have passed since he had last engaged in the dance of procuring himself a bed partner, but it had not been that long, *by God*. And some things a man was not capable of erasing from his memory.

"Of course." She smiled, but it did not reach her eyes. "Winchelsea. I am not a naïve young girl. I know what you want."

His heart beat faster, and a chill trilled down his spine. She could not know who he was or what his true intentions were. Surely not. "Oh? I pray you enlighten me, Mademoiselle Beaumont. What is it I want?"

She stepped closer to him, her red silk swaying against his trousers. "You want me."

Want more? *Scandalous Duke* is available now!

Don't miss Scarlett's other romances!

(Listed by Series)

Complete Book List
scarlettscottauthor.com/books

HISTORICAL ROMANCE

Heart's Temptation
A Mad Passion (Book One)
Rebel Love (Book Two)
Reckless Need (Book Three)
Sweet Scandal (Book Four)
Restless Rake (Book Five)
Darling Duke (Book Six)
The Night Before Scandal (Book Seven)

Wicked Husbands
Her Errant Earl (Book One)
Her Lovestruck Lord (Book Two)
Her Reformed Rake (Book Three)
Her Deceptive Duke (Book Four)
Her Missing Marquess (Book Five)

League of Dukes
Nobody's Duke (Book One)
Heartless Duke (Book Two)
Dangerous Duke (Book Three)
Shameless Duke (Book Four)
Scandalous Duke (Book Five)
Fearless Duke (Book Six)

Sins and Scoundrels
Duke of Depravity (Book One)
Prince of Persuasion (Book Two)
Marquess of Mayhem (Book Three)
Earl of Every Sin (Book Four)

The Wicked Winters
Wicked in Winter (Book One)
Wedded in Winter (Book Two)
Wanton in Winter (Book Three)
Willful in Winter (Book Four)
Wagered in Winter (Book Five)
Wild in Winter (Book Six)

Stand-alone Novella
Lord of Pirates

CONTEMPORARY ROMANCE

Love's Second Chance
Reprieve (Book One)
Perfect Persuasion (Book Two)
Win My Love (Book Three)

Coastal Heat
Loved Up (Book One)

About the Author

USA Today and Amazon bestselling author Scarlett Scott writes steamy Victorian and Regency romance with strong, intelligent heroines and sexy alpha heroes. She lives in Pennsylvania with her Canadian husband, adorable identical twins, and one TV-loving dog.

A self-professed literary junkie and nerd, she loves reading anything, but especially romance novels, poetry, and Middle English verse. Catch up with her on her website www.scarlettscottauthor.com. Hearing from readers never fails to make her day.

Scarlett's complete book list and information about upcoming releases can be found at www.scarlettscottauthor.com.

Connect with Scarlett! You can find her here:
Join Scarlett Scott's reader's group on Facebook for early excerpts, giveaways, and a whole lot of fun!
Sign up for her newsletter here.
scarlettscottauthor.com/contact
Follow Scarlett on Amazon
Follow Scarlett on BookBub
www.instagram.com/scarlettscottauthor
www.twitter.com/scarscoromance
www.pinterest.com/scarlettscott
www.facebook.com/AuthorScarlettScott
Join the Historical Harlots on Facebook